# THROUGH
# FIRE AND WATER

### By Avi Schwartz

## ACKNOWLEDGEMENTS

The book is dedicated to my Mother, Henya Harriet, of Blessed Memory, who taught me about unconditional love.
My heroic Father, Mordechai, who constantly teaches me about self-sacrifice,
and to the Creator of Heaven and Earth for allowing me to write this story of Redemption.
I also want to acknowledge Tressa Janik, my editor, who encouraged me with her enthusiasm to see the story unfold.
Last of all, special thanks to Andre Cowell, who, upon hearing the storyline, insisted I write the book.

# Chapter 1

Night had ended as the sun was appearing over the Manhattan skyline and still Michael Winston was no closer to saving his kidnapped father, Jake. Jake was an old, frail, and decorated World War II war hero, whose fate now lay in his son's hands. Only five days remained until the month long deadline. Throughout the harrowing night, he was manipulated into running fifty blocks, desperately racing from ringing pay phone to pay phone, answering the calls on time, fulfilling the sadistic demands of Simon, the ringmaster of the whole operation. Simon taunted and played with him like a mouse caught in a trap. With his lungs burning from exhaustion, he managed to answer another one.

"How many times do I have to tell you? This is not a game", said Simon.

"What do you think I am doing? Fooling around? I am doing my best", pleaded Michael.

"Your best", retorted Simon. "Tell that to your father when we send him to hell."

"Let me talk to my father", yelled Michael. "Let me--"

Simon hung up, leaving Michael with only the dial tone.

Frustrated, Michael banged the receiver.

"Please. Please."

From the side of his eye he noticed a homeless man walking up the sidewalk, pushing a shopping cart. "Sid. Sid", shouted Michael.

"Who wants to know?"

Unfamiliar with Michael's cleaned up and well-dressed look, Sid couldn't recognize him.

"It's me. Mike. Michael. Mikey."

"Mikey? What happened to you?"

"They got my father! They're going to take him down."

Off in the distance another pay phone was ringing.

"You got to help me, Sid. You got to."

Michael reached into his right hand jacket pocket, removed a digital recorder, and handed it over to him.

Another pay phone rang, chiming in harmony with the first phone. "It's all here. I got to go."

Michael gave chase. Sid activated the recorder.

Sounds of ferocious thunder, heavy rain, blustering wind, and Michael wailing were heard. It was the night that his father died, twenty-five days earlier.

Several hours had passed since Jake had passed on. The grief was infusing itself into Michael. A failed but brilliant man, Michael had been living on the streets for the last fifteen years. Homeless, his only companion was his shopping cart, "Marty". Overwhelmed with loss, pangs of guilt and self-loathing he raced through Central Park numb to the wild and dark storm. One could barely see him.

Lightning struck the cart, revealing a half crazed man, with disheveled hair, a long unkempt beard, and a digital recorder tied to a strap hanging around his neck. The fifteen years had taken their toll on Michael.

The lightning bolt overturned the cart, spilling its contents to the ground. In the center of the mess laid a framed photograph of a younger Michael, in a college cap and gown, arm in arm with his father, a gentle but powerful man.

Estranged from his father, Michael had never stopped thinking about him and how he let him down. The

7

photograph was the only item left that reminded him of his glory days and the future that he had hoped to achieve but was now lost, since his father would never see his son succeed.

As if his life force was in the balance, he quickly picked up the photo and kissed it. "Oh Pops. Pops."

The ground began to shake wildly. An immense and menacing shadow quickly approached as the ground split. Michael hastily returned the contents into the shopping cart and began running for his life. A towering wall shot out from the underneath, followed by three more, trapping him. A beam of light descended and whisked him upwards and through a tunnel that seemed to traverse billions of light years and worlds away, bringing him into a dark oval room.

Standing in the center of the room, he began pacing back and forth, trying to overcome his fear as he calmed himself down by talking into his recorder.

"Where am I?"

A very bright spotlight shined into his face.

Behind the spotlight, an unseen mysterious figure had commenced to speak. It was Simon.

"Silence. Michael Winston. Silence. We have your father", said Simon.

"My father? My father? You're crazier than I am. My father is dead."

"Maybe in your world. But this is the Hereafter. Look."

Appearing on the wall was a myriad of downcast human beings, in black outfits, marching in uniform lines toward a horrible inferno.

Among them was Jake.

"Pops! Pops!"

Running towards the image he was hurled back by a

force field sending him across the room.

"Let my father go!" Let my father go!"

The room's door opened. Standing in the doorway, with a whip in hand, cracking it against the floor, was the tall and looming figure of Mr. Benjamin. Supposedly he was Jake Winston's defending angel.

"Thank you, Mr. Simon. I'll take over from here", said Mr. Benjamin.

"Very good. Mr. Benjamin."

Making eye contact with Michael, Mr. Benjamin began whipping Michael, causing him to pull back.

"Scared, Michael? Terrified? I don't know whose more a coward, you or your pathetic father?" said Mr. Benjamin.

"No one calls my father a coward. No one."

Uncontrollable with anger and impervious to the lashes, he charged Mr. Benjamin.

Immediately the guards rushed into the room, restraining Michael.

"Sit him down."

"Listen carefully to me, Mr. Winston. Your father is here because he deserves to be."

"No. No. My father is a good man, a kind man. He has helped so many people."

Then Mr. Joseph entered, holding the folder of Michael's father's life. Encircling Michael like a cat after its prey, he flipped through the folder.

"I wouldn't upset Mr. Benjamin if I were you", remarked Mr. Joseph. "He may be an angel but he's no sweetheart. Play along. Tell him he's right...that your father is a coward. It will make him feel better."

"What are you? Nuts?"

"No. But you are." snarled Mr. Benjamin.

"This isn't real. Guilt. Guilt." Michael told himself.

"I am having a guilt attack. I should have visited Pops."

Fifteen years of guilt had come crashing down on Michael. He knew that this time he had crossed the line by not visiting Pops one last time as he was dying in the hospital. He truly was a failure as a son and as a man.

"I'm afraid this is no illusion, Mr. Winston", said Mr. Benjamin, imitating Rod Serling. "Welcome to the Corridor of Judgment."

Overwhelming fear gripped Michael as the Twilight Zone theme played in the background. His breathing became heavy, his heart beat wildly fast, and his head was pounding.

"The Corridor of Judgment, the last exit before Hell. It is a place where the soul of man meets its moment of reckoning. The point of no return. Where action and consequence merge into Heaven or Hell. You have entered the Corridor of Judgment."

"Thank you, Mr. Benjamin." quipped Mr. Joseph. "Well, Mr. Winston. This is the point of no return. And within another few moments your father's fate will arrive at that point."

Nearly beside himself, swaying back and forth, Michael was near a nervous breakdown.

"This is not going to work. He's insane. The panel is not going to go for this", said Mr. Benjamin.

"Look. I'm his father's guardian angel", said Mr. Joseph.

Catching them off guard, Simon's unseen voice spoke. "Time is up, Mr. Joseph."

Mr. Winston pleaded frantically with Mr. Joseph. "What's it going to be? Heaven or Hell?" Confounded by this surreal moment Michael was mumbling, "Heaven or Hell. Heaven or Hell." Alarms then sounded off as a monstrous bright warning light came on.

"Decide!" yelled Mr. Joseph. "Decide."

"Heaven! Heaven!" Shouted Michael.

Turning to Simon, Mr. Joseph yelled, "Heaven! He is going to do it! He is going to do it!"

Immediately the alarms stopped.

"Do what?" asked Michael.

"Mr. Benjamin", said Mr. Joseph. "The watch. Please."

Mr. Benjamin removed a stopwatch from within his jacket and handed it over. Quickly Mr. Joseph placed it on Michael's wrist.

"Time is of the essence, Mr. Winston", said Mr. Joseph. "Do you understand?"

"Essence, to what? Time is of the essence? To what?"

"Your father's eternal life. Haven't you been listening?" asked Mr. Joseph.

Upset with Michael's lack of understanding, Mr. Benjamin grabbed him by the lapel of his jacket.

"Listen." said Mr. Benjamin. "You good for nothing bum, you see this stopwatch? you have thirty days to save your father's life. No more. No less. You see. It is set to zero days. Zero hours. Zero seconds."

Mr. Benjamin then activated it. "It has officially begun." forcefully remarked Mr. Benjamin.

Now there was no going back. Everything now lay in Michael's hands.

Suddenly the alarm system sounded off as Mr. Reuben, a somewhat elderly angel, known as the Prosecutor, entered the room.

"Guards! Place Mr. Joseph and Mr. Benjamin under arrest."

"On what charge?" Protested Mr. Joseph.

"Omission of Information!" forcefully exclaimed Mr. Reuben.

"What omission? Mr. Winston is a mentally ill man. There is no way he has the wherewithal to withstand the test", answered Mr. Reuben.

Seeing there was no choice, Mr. Joseph signaled Mr. Benjamin with his eyes, hinting to charge Mr. Reuben. Quickly they lunged forward and began choking him.

The guards immediately encircled both of them drawing their weapons.

"Everybody stand back", yelled Mr. Joseph.

Turning to Michael, Mr. Benjamin commanded him. "Mr. Winston. Get ready to beam down."

"To Earth? To Life? Forget it. It's hell down there."

"You see my point." Mr. Reuben said gasping for air. "The poor man already forgot about his father. How do you expect him to save him?"

Two unseen guards, standing in the rear of Mr. Reuben, lunged forward and overpowered both Mr. Joseph and Mr. Benjamin. "My father...that's right...My father. I got to save Pops", remembered Michael.

"Tap the watch!" shouted Mr. Joseph.

Tapping it, nothing happened.

"Tap it harder...Hit the watch! Just hit it!"

Michael did and the same tunnel of light that brought Mike to Heaven reappeared.

"Guards! Grab him!" yelled Mr. Reuben.

"Mike," commanded Mr. Joseph. "Jump into the light! Jump!"

Michael jumped into it and within moments he was back in Central Park standing in the raging storm. "I got to save Pops! How?" railed Michael. "You didn't tell me, how!"

# Chapter 2

Morning had now arrived and all was calm.

Mike was lying on the ground, fast asleep, clutching onto the photo of his father and himself. Beside him was "Marty".

The stopwatch alarm sounded off slightly, waking up Michael. The moment he opened his eyes the alarm stopped. But Michael was too mentally and emotionally exhausted to remain awake. Quickly he fell asleep. For the next minutes this sequence of actions occurred - the alarm ringing, Mike wup, the alarm stopping, and then him returning to sleep. Michael had forgotten about his mission.

Then without any warning every alarm clock in the city sounded off, causing Mike to jump to his feet. He was dazed and confused.

Looking down at his left wrist he noticed the stopwatch. 29 DAYS. 9 HOURS. 14 SECONDS REMAINING.

The sight of the watch triggered his memory.

"Time is of the essence...that's what Mr. Benjamin said. What to do? I need to talk to Charlie."

With Marty in hand he began running towards the Lower East Side, where his old college friend, Charlie Gates, was shooting a movie.

Mike and Charlie had been the top NYU film students. Creative, intelligent, and hard-working, they were viewed as the new wave of up and coming filmmakers. Especially, Mike. He was regarded as the new Orson Welles-- extremely innovative, profoundly intelligent and extraordinarily talented. "A true genius" as Charlie called him.

Twenty years had passed since those days. Charlie had become the world famous auteur, producing masterpieces and breaking box office records as Mike slowly regressed, becoming the mad genius of the Bowery. Respectfully and always in awe of his friend's talent, and heartbroken at Michael's breakdown, Charlie made sure that Michael always had access to him and his sets.

Arriving at the location, he ran into the closed-off city block, bringing the in-progress shoot to a halt. It was an occurrence the crew had become accustomed.

"Where's Charlie?"

The production assistants pointed towards video village, the area where the director and his immediate crew sat behind the video assist watching the scene as it was filmed.

"Charlie!"

With a slight smile Charlie turned to his old friend.

"Yeah, Mike."

"I got to talk to you now. Now...In the trailer!"

Mike turning to the assistant director Charlie quietly said, "Everybody, take five."

Now in the trailer Charlie noticed Mike's clothes dripping wet.

"You're soaked!"

"Never mind that! Just listen. You're not going to believe this. What do you know about the Corridor of Judgment?"

"Did you call your mom, yet? It's almost been a week now since I told you about your father."

14

Mike was shamefaced to tell him he did not call.

"She needs you, especially now. Come on, Mike."

"I will..."

"Anyhow, what about the Corridor of Judgment?" Charlie asked.

"You heard of it?"

Charlie smiled.

"How does it work?"

"Don't ask me." Answered Charlie. "You created it. It's your script. Corridor of Judgment.NYU,student film twenty years ago? Remember?"

"Yeah. Then how do you explain this?" Mike pointed to the stopwatch. "It is gone. Where is the watch? I lost the watch. I need the watch."

"Relax Mike." said Charlie. "Take it easy. Take mine." Slowly Mike realized that he was hallucinating."

"Corridor of Judgment...Charlie...where guilt and failure emerge into nightmare... What was I thinking, long ago and far away? Dreams of an aspiring filmmaker? Hey Charlie?"

"Don't worry about it, Mike. Your are very grief-stricken about your father. Let's go shoot a scene."

Back on set and in the video village Michael was in his milieu, ordering the crew and actors. Though everyone felt they were in the presence of cinematic greatness, they were apprehensive to listen.

"You heard the genius." Charlie commanded the director of photography. "Do it."

Just then the nearby pay phones started ringing, one after the other, in quick succession.

"Where the hell are the production assistants? Can someone please get the phones?" yelled Mike.

A blaring siren sounded off; it was emanating from Mike's left wrist. The stopwatch had reappeared.

"This isn't real."

Desperately trying to ignore this hallucination, he struggled to direct the scene.

"Go tight and then pan. But do it in a waltz rhythm...ok...Lets shoot this..."

He began speaking to himself trying to reinforce his sense of self. "I am not mad...I can do this...Just focus, Mike. Focus."

When he refused to heed the alarm, the stopwatch sent him an electric current, jolting Mike.

"What the hell is going on here?"

Shocked from the jolt he turned to look at the stopwatch.

"ANSWER THE PHONE!" read the screen.

"That's it." Yelled Michael. "I am out of here."

Leaving the set and the crew confused, Michael took Marty and ran towards the phone. Answering it.

"The tests begin, Mr. Winston", said the eerie voice of Simon. "Now. Turn around. What do you see?"

"A bus", answered Michael.

"Look down the avenue. What do you see?"

"A gas station."

"Good. In one minute, two of its tires are going to blow out and the bus is going to crash into the gas pumps resulting in death and destruction."

"This isn't happening." Mike told himself.

"Oh. It is. You have less than a minute to stop the unfortunate accident and save their lives."

"I am going nuts here."

"Stop the bus, Mr. Winston! Their lives and your father's life depend on it."

"Marty. You hear this. I'm losing it...Mind over matter...I...Close your eyes Michael." he said to himself.

He closed his eyes only to quickly reopen them,

16

hearing the bus' tires blow out. His sight was transfixed on the out of control bus heading right into the gas pumps, exploding on impact.

Responding to the fiery explosion pedestrians and the film crew tried to help. "I told you, Mr. Winston. Why didn't you listen?" forcefully said Simon.

"What did I do?"

Overwhelmed Michael fell to the ground.

"Get up, Mr. Winston...Get up. So many lives...And you could have saved them, too bad for them and your father. As Mr. Joseph said, 'time is of the essence'...Next test...Twenty-Third Street and Canal."

"What about it?" a distraught Mike asked.

"Five minutes. That's all you got. Hopefully, you'll do better this time."

"What's going to happen? Hello! Hello!"

Simon had hung the phone up.

"Oh no. Oh no. Twenty-third Street and Canal.... Come on Marty."

Pushing Marty he ran down the streets, weaving in and out of crossing pedestrians and vehicles.

Out of breath he slowed down for a minute, but the stopwatch immediately reacted with powerful deep bass beeps in one-second intervals and a computer-generated voice announcing the countdown.

With only fifty-nine seconds remaining Michael took a large grasp of air and continued running.

Arriving at 23rd Street and Canal, Michael scanned the area. All he saw was a kid's baseball game in progress and the regular movement of a busy New York street.

"Fifteen seconds and counting.", announced the stopwatch.

The boy at bat hit a long fly ball sending it past the outfield and towards the street. Chasing after the ball the

17

left outfielder ran through a makeshift opening in the surrounding fence and headed into the street.

Bending to pick up the ball a large unseen delivery truck was making a turn. The driver was occupied with flipping the radio channels to notice.

"Watch out!" yelled Michael. "Watch out for the truck!"

"Three seconds and counting...." announced the watch. "Two seconds and counting...One second and counting..."

Michael sprinted towards the boy.

"Watch ouuuuuuuuuut!", frantically yelled Michael.

"J.J." his friends screamed. "There is a truck. A truck."

The driver noticed the boy and braked with all his power and skill, screeching to a halt. But it was too late. The truck hit the boy. Screeching to a halt, the driver jumped out.

"No. No." cried Michael.

Everyone seemed to move in slow motion, completely in shock.

A nearby phone rang. Reeling with shock, Mike somehow found the strength to turn towards the phone and answer it. "You shouldn't have slowed down before.", said Simon. "Why the kid? He was just a kid", a guilt-ridden Michael cried. "What did he ever do wrong?" Simon hung up, leaving Michael alone to sink into soul-searching remorse.

# CHAPTER 3

Several hours had passed. Walking up Midtown Avenue, he looked at his watch, wondering if he hadn't stopped to rest could he have really saved the little boy.

Failure had become Michael's lot in life, but until now it was only he who had to suffer the consequences. Never before had his weakness affected others.

Exhausted, he was about to lie down on the pavement and get some rest, only to be disturbed by a ringing pay phone again. But this time he had learned his lesson. Simon meant business.

He ran to the phone.

"Hello...Where have you been? I can't take this tension..."

There was no answer.

"Hello...Do you hear me? Hello." said Michael.

The call went to dial tone.

"Hello. Great...wrong number."

Hanging up the phone he started walking away. Halfway down the block the phone rang again. He stopped, assessed the situation and walked back. About to answer the phone the ringing stopped.

Frustrated he paused a moment, and began walking away. Again the phone rang. This time he had it. He was going to end Simon's sadistic game. Running back he lifted the phone and yelled.

"Hello...Hello...I said hello. Either speak or..."

"Michael.... Michael."

"Pops!", said a surprised Michael. He was floored

hearing his father, Jake's, sweet voice. No matter what, his father's voice always comforted Michael. Bursting into tears, he had realized how deeply he missed his beloved father and how he disappointed him.

"Pops! I am so...."

"Michael.", said a tearing Jake. "Don't worry Mikey."

"Yeah Pops...I knew you'd get away."

"You did a good job, Mickey."

"You saw that? I let the bus crash...I let the boy die."

"It was out of your hands. At least you tried."

"I miss you."

"I miss you, Mike...It's good to hear your voice again. Listen. Whatever they give you, whatever Simon gives you; you can handle it. Remember that."

"I don't know Pops. It's like Malibu all over again."

"Let go of me", yelled Jake.

Hearing a commotion on his father's end Michael shouted, "What's going on Pops?"

"Take your hands off me", continued Jake.

"Time's up, Mr. Winston", said Simon. "Take him away."

Simon had brought Jake to the phone to tease and torment Michael.

Michael could hear his father being dragged away protesting.

"Leave my father alone. Leave him alone."

"Contain yourself, Mr. Winston. Contain yourself."

Michael calmed down.

"That's better. Rest...Good. You'll need your energy. As you can see we still have your father. Do you understand? I said do you understand?"

"Yeah. I understand." an angry Mike said.

"Good...Corner of Thirtieth and..."

20

Then static came on the line making it impossible to hear the number of the avenue.

"Now." said Simon hanging the phone.

"Thirtieth and what? Thirtieth and what? West side or east side...come on you son of a..."

He looked at his watch hoping to obtain more information. Pushing all the buttons nothing appeared.

"Damn it! Damn it!"

The watch alarm began beeping its warning mode.

"Come on Marty."

Grabbing Marty he started running towards Thirtieth Street, cutting through traffic and pedestrians.

# CHAPTER 4

Arriving at Thirtieth Street and Fifth Avenue, out of breath he scanned the horizon not knowing which direction. With every passing moment the alarm grew louder.

"Great. Just great." he frustratingly said. "You see this Marty...." Upset, he reached into his pocket and pulled out a coin. "Heads, west side. Tails, east side."

He flipped the coin.

"West side it is."

About to take off, he paused for a moment, thinking of a faster way to move. Quickly he rummaged through his cart and pulled out a pair of roller blades.

"Who says you can't skate through life, hey, Marty?"

He placed on the blades and took off with Marty, blading down the west side along the Hudson River. Looking at each corner, he saw New York being just New York: busy with traffic, honking cabbies, tourists, New Yorkers, cyclists, and joggers.

"I don't see anything", he yelled heavenward. "Thirtieth and what?"

Again he played with the watch. Suddenly it spoke.

"Thirtieth and First."

"You couldn't tell me before.... You couldn't tell me this before...Thirtieth and First...What? Do you know how far that is?" "Two and a half miles.", said the watch.

"Thank you," said Michael.

"You're welcome." said the watch.

22

Michael did a double take, surprised at the watch's courtesy. "Alright...no time..."

Rummaging through the cart he pulled out various badges.

"Fire? No good. Building Inspector? No good. Security for the Mayor's office? No good. Detective? Good. "

Continuing to rummage he pulled out a gun and fired it, squirting out water. It was a toy water gun he carried for protection. Placing his hands into the cart he pulled out a rope.

"Alright, Marty. Watch this."

He rollerbladed with Marty to a traffic light and flashed his detective badge and gun at a slow moving cab driven by an Indian cabbie.

"Pull Over! Pull Over. Police business. Undercover."

Apprehensive the cabbie pulled over.

Quickly Michael securely tied the rope to the cab's rear bumper and to Marty. "Thirtieth and First. Now! Hi! Ho! Silver away!"

"What?" asked the cabbie?

"Lets go! Get me to Thirtieth and First!"

Afraid to resist an officer the cabbie took off.

"That's it. Hi. Ho Silver away!", shouted Michael.

Passing through traffic Mike kept up with the speeding cab, revealing skill and agility as he maneuvered pass various obstacles. From time to time Michael would yell out, "Hi. Ho. Silver away!", which was enthusiastically repeated by the cabbie, who became an instant fan of Michael's skills and courage.

"We're here!", yelled the cabbie, as they arrived at Thirtieth and First.

Mike untied the rope.

"Thanks...You did a fine job, citizen.", said Michael.

"Welcome...Thank you...Hi. Ho Silver Way away.",
shouted the cabbie as he pulled away.

Looking for anything suspicious, Michael caught
sight of two hooded men with guns, carrying money bags
and running out of the corner bank towards an awaiting
getaway car parked nearby scaffolding. The scaffolding
was unstable.

The stopwatch announced, "Danger! Danger!
Danger!"

"Ah. Damn. This is the next test. Isn't it?", nervously
said Michael.

Assessing the area before he took any action, he saw a
mailbox. It was the only object that could provide him
cover. Pointing his gun and badge, he mustered the
courage and yelled.

"Police. Stop. Or I will shoot."

Hearing the warning the bankers turned and fired
their guns. Michael quickly ran towards the mailbox.

Panic ensued as the pedestrians ran for cover behind
parked cars, food vendors, hotel revolving doors and
hitting the pavement.

Traffic came to a halt, blocking the banking bankers
near the scaffolding.

"Come on, Mike. Think, man! Think Man!" he yelled
at himself.

He caught sight of the Indian cabbie. He repeatedly
shouted at the top of his lungs, "Hi. Ho Silver Away," until
he caught the cabbie's attention.

Making eye contact Michael pointed towards the
shaky scaffolding. Gesturing with hand signals he
instructed the cabbie to ram his vehicle into the
scaffolding.

Understanding the instructions, the cabbie took his
anti-theft club, placed it on the gas pedal, shifted into

drive, drove towards the scaffolding, and jumped out of the car just in the nick of time, yelling, "Hi. Ho. Silver away!" The impact of the speeding cab brought the scaffolding crashing down on the getaway car, ending the gunfire.

A moment later the area was swarmed with police cars.

Glancing at the stopwatch, a message was sent. "Not bad, but not a Lifesaver. Delancy Subway Station! Now! Simon."

"This is coercion.", yelled Michael. "Coercion."

"Ok. Come on, Marty.", angrily said Michael.

# CHAPTER 5

Reaching the Delancy Subway Station, Michael saw it was busy with riders entering and exiting the station. Nervous to leave Marty alone, he knew he had no choice; it was just too cumbersome to take with him into the station.

"Just stay here, Marty." Leaving Marty at the top of the stairs he ran down.

Landing at the bottom, he passed Joey, a homeless and deranged man that Michael had known for several years. Joey was leaning against a pillar, bemoaning the evil ways of womanhood. Nearly ten years had passed since his ex-wife, Andrea, left him. The abandonment and its aftermath had wrecked his life.

"Beware woman! She will trap you. Interrogate you. Steal your soul from you. And tell you it is you to blame.", was his daily chant. A chant he repeated all day long at every arriving train and its exiting and boarding passengers.

Two pillars away from Joey was a beautiful woman, Lisa Hoffman, a marketing director. She regularly took the same train at this station. She had grown accustomed to Joey's rants.

Meanwhile unable to see anything that seemed to look like danger Michael turned to his stopwatch. It was gone. "Where is the watch? I am such an idiot!"

Immediately he began to re-trace his steps. Down the platform was Joey.

"Ain't I right? Beautiful woman?", Joey yelled towards Lisa. Politely she smiled and turned the other way. "Hey, Joey...Hey, Joey. Did you see a watch?" nervously questioned Mike.

"Oh, hi, Mike."

"Did you see a watch?"

Dazed and in his own world Joey just stared at Michael and walked away, revealing an engraving on the pillar. It was an inscription that pierced Michael like an arrow between his eyes, "CORRIDOR OF JUDGEMENT. MIKE AND CHARLIE - WELLES AND HOUSTON - EAT YOUR HEART OUT".

"Corridor of Judgment? What the hell is happening to me? I carved that out nearly twenty years ago."

Michael realized that his inner torment over his father was just a self-created ploy and that he had hallucinated himself into a heroic fantasy. There was no watch. No alarms. No challenges. He was acting out a movie plot he created. It was the only way he could live with himself. The days of opportunity whereby he could bring pride to his beloved father were gone.

Dejected, he walked up the staircase heading towards the street level. Meanwhile, Joey was nervously pacing back and forth, inching closer to Lisa. At the top of the stairs, the deep bass sound of alarm beeps began again.

"Ninety seconds and counting.... Eighty-five seconds and counting" said the stopwatch's voice.

Michael slapped his face in attempt to stop the hallucination.

"Stop it. Mike. Stop it. Pops is gone. You blew it. Live with it." he told himself, trying to hold back his tears.

"What the hell was wrong with me all these years?"

Reaching the top of the staircase he looked at the only friend he had left, Marty. Gently and slowly he pushed Marty down the block, ignoring both the sounds and voices of his mind. Oblivious he nearly bumped into a young mother and her five-year old son.

"Come on, David.", said the young mother. "Don't stare. It's not nice. Just keeping walking."

"Well, mommy. If the man would just lower the alarm on his stopwatch he would be able to concentrate on his walking.", said the little boy.

"What did you just say, kid?" said Michael. "You hear the alarm?"

"Yeah. Turn it down."

"Where is the watch?"

"It's on your left wrist."

Mike looked and saw the watch on his wrist.

"What color is it?" questioned Michael, trying to find out if the boy was legitimate.

"Blue."

"Simon. You son of.... You tried to play with me."

Quickly turning around he ran back to the station, left Marty at the top of the subway entrance, and headed downstairs.

With every step he ran along the platform the countdown got louder and louder, yet still he saw no danger.

Trains were entering and leaving the station.

"Fifteen seconds and counting." announced the watch.

Dumbstruck he turned towards the carving on the pillar. Self-doubt had crept inside him again. Wanting to get some sense of bearing he turned to Joey. It was the only person he knew at the station.

28

Staring at Joey, he didn't notice that Joey was standing behind Lisa, repeatedly calling out for "Andrea". Joey had become fixated on Lisa. He thought she was Andrea.

"You didn't have to leave me. I tried to save our marriage. I did everything you asked. I loved you Andrea. You said I was the love of your life. The love of your life."

The rumbling of an arriving train could be heard as the wind in the tunnel grew strong and its headlight could be seen reflecting off the wall.

"Five. Four. Three. Two. One." announced the watch.

"It's over Andrea. Over.", said Joey as he suddenly pushed Lisa to the tracks.
Desperate commuters helpless to assist tried to flag down the train but it was too late.
"Oh! My God, Simon! What did you do?" yelled Mike.

Immediately Mike jumped onto the tracks and ran towards Lisa as the train conductor sounded the whistle and tried to brake.

Reaching Lisa, he grabbed and pulled her into the track's open space, pressing her and himself against the track wall as the train passed them.

The train had come to a screeching halt.

The commuters and the arriving transit police looked into the tracks searching for two bodies.

Emerging from the tracks was Michael and Lisa, both alive. Lisa was slightly bruised from the fall.

Overwhelmed with gratitude, Lisa turned to look at the hero who risked his life to save her.

"I want to thank you so much."

Dumfounded, Mike could not speak.

"What's your name?"

He was looking into the eyes of the only woman he ever loved. Twenty years earlier, they were to marry but his obsession with becoming the next great Hollywood artist drove a wedge between them.

He thought to himself, "Damn you, Simon. You trapped my father. You sent me on a crazy mission. And now you bring me to Lisa. What kind of bastard are you? How can I tell her my name? Look at me. I am a bum. A bum."

Looking deeply into her eyes, he turned his face down in shame as he walked away, ignoring the paramedics that just arrived.

# Chapter 6

Several hours had passed and no message had arrived from Simon. With each succeeding step Michael took pushing Marty along Eighth Avenue, he could remember the desperate moments of his life, when he reached rock bottom, feeling completely abandoned and betrayed by the people he loved and trusted. Until she left, Lisa had been the anchor of his young adult life. She was a budding student architect and he was set to recreate cinema. Seeing her again forced him to contemplate why they broke up? Something he had not done in over 15 years. For years he tormented himself about why she left him. All he could hear in his mind was her complaints. He was too demanding. Too tough! Too everything. He wasn't emotionally available for her.

The day was now nearing its end as the sun was setting over the Manhattan skyline, and still no word. Michael was nearly collapsing with worry, fatigue, and the constant mental replay of his encounter with Lisa.

Then the watch vibrated with a text message.

"WELL DONE, MR. WINSTON. WE APPRECIATE YOUR EFFORTS. BUT THE RULING BODY HAS FOUND YOUR FATHER GUILTY. THANK YOU. BEST IN YOUR FUTURE ENDEAVORS."

"What the hell is that? You can't do this? This is not fair! What is my father guilty of?"

The torment he had known before was extreme but

now those fires within his soul had taken him to a new low.

"Give me a second chance. What are you doing to me? What kind of creatures are you? They are killing me, Marty."

Leaving Marty on the sidewalk, he walked into traffic. He was ready to die.

Cars and trucks were blowing their horns, yet nothing budged Michael. A vehicle was coming up the avenue and heading into Michael's direction.

"Is that the way you want to play it, Simon?", he yelled heavenward. "You got it. You condemn my father. My death will condemn you. If my father is going to Hell, then you are going with him. I won't move unless I get a fair hearing."

"Simon! My father will see you in Hell."

Just as the oncoming car was about to impact the same beam of light that earlier transported Michael descended and whisked him upwards through the tunnel and brought him to Mr. Levy's conference room. He was Jake Winston's defense lawyer. It was bustling with angelic lawyers, wearing business suits, furiously gathering information, preparing his father's case. They were huddled around a large round table, strewn with documents, files, and records of various aspects of Jake Winston's life.

Mr. Levy was mustached, and always wore a three-piece suit, which was unusual for a celestial being. But ever since he saw Clarence Darrow, the famed trial lawyer, back in the 1920s he felt a kinship with his style and manner, and so switched to the same apparel as Darrow. This caused much resentment among many of the other Celestial lawyers. They felt humiliated that a human being would influence a Celestial being. But that

32

is what made him so effective. He had studied human behavior and its abhorrent condition. He had seen the evolution of Man. He had seen all types saints, murderers, thieves, jilted lovers, bullies, artists, rulers, and drug addicts. But nothing perplexed him more than the fact that Celestial beings came into existence on Day Two, while Man on Day Six, and yet Man behaved like an inferior creation. He always felt that Man received a raw deal, being both composed of earthly and divine elements. It was a stacked deck.

"Where's the World War II file?" Mr. Levy requested of his staff. "Could someone please get me the file? We go to the hearing in less than three minutes."

Michael was bewildered by their speed and stop motion movement. They moved like a wave and particle. Moving in and out of dimensions of time and space. It was if wormholes, black holes, and sub-atomic reality were all fused in one location and these beings were moving without restraint.

Turning to Michael, Mr. Levy called him over. "Michael. Michael."

"Yes sir," said a startled Michael.

Mr. Levy gestured him to approach.

"You were quite impressive today. My name is Mr. Levy. I am your father's defense lawyer." Mr. Levy's assistant, Mr. Aaron, brought the file.

"Here, Sir."

"Thank you."

Skimming through it, he repeatedly nodded his head.

"Um... very good. Excellent. Now I see where you get your courage. Time to go."

Somewhat relaxed, Michael followed Mr. Levy into the corridor that led to the Justice Hall of the Universe. Here is where all the three hundred and ten universes were scrutinized, analyzed, and judged. Sometimes the judges sat as a board, judging the new universes as if they were a start-up company. But today was different. Today a human being was going to be judged. And so above the Hall's enormous doors was engraved, "MEASURE FOR MEASURE SHALL BE METED OUT TO ALL".

Justice Hall was grand in size, an arch-laden edifice with high ceilings with the scales of Justice mounted over the empty seated Judges' dais. The gallery was packed to capacity with onlookers, anxiously waiting to view this unprecedented hearing. Never before had the Heavenly Court heard an appeal on a closed case.

Mr. Levy and Michael took their assigned seats at the defense table along the already seated Mr. Joseph and Mr. Benjamin. Their lives also hung in the balance. Sitting across at the persecution table was Mr. Reuben and his team.

The Court Officer had approached and commenced to announce in a grand and commanding style bringing an instant hush over the Justice Hall.

"Hear ye. Hear ye. The Right Honorable Court of Celestial Beings is hereby convened. All rise as the esteemed Panel of Five take the bench."

As the Panel of Five entered the court room, Michael was taken aback by the stern and imposing figures of the Justices, especially Chief Justice Daniel. His piercing blue steel eyes seemed like it could penetrate anyone's hidden agendas.

"Case number 25992 shall now be heard.", announced the court officer.

Chief Justice Daniel looked sternly at both sides setting the tone to the serious nature of the moment.

34

"As we all know", he said, "this is a hearing and not a trial. Nonetheless, this hearing is unprecedented. Never have officers of the court, namely Mr. Joseph and Mr. Benjamin, have so flagrantly displayed such open contempt to the rules of Celestial proceeding as they have done."

"Chief Justice Daniel.", interrupted Mr. Levy. "Forgive me for interrupting, but since this is a hearing and not a trial why has Your Honor already slanted the...."

"Slanted!", angrily quipped Chief Justice Daniel. "Are you implying what I think you are, Mr. Levy?"

"No sir. I am not implying. Rather I'm stating unequivocally. The opening remarks of the panel are slanted."

Everyone was shocked at Mr. Levy's accusation.

"You are out of order sir." blasted Chief Justice Daniel.

"Out of order...the phrase belongs to trial proceeding and not to a hearing. There can be no doubt! The panel is slanted." Upset, nonetheless the Chief Justice held himself back.

"Based on your remarks it clearly seems to the panel of five that the contempt displayed by Mister Joseph and Benjamin is in keeping with their superior, namely you, Mr. Levy. Hence, the hearing panel has heard all it needs to hear concerning Mister Joseph and Benjamin and the fate of Mr. Jake Winston. Therefore, this hearing is hereby adjourned. Good day."

Justice Hall turned into pandemonium at the lack of due process.

"What is going on here?" demanded Michael.

The Court bailiffs approached and took Mr. Joseph and Benjamin into custody.

"I am truly sorry", said Mr. Joseph to Michael.

"That's it? Over? What about my father?"

"I tried." Mr. Levy said in a resigned voice.

"You tried? You tried? Heaven. Earth. You lawyers are all the same. What about the file? Show them the file!" demanded Michael.

"It's too late," retorted Mr. Levy.

"Show them the file."

"I'm sorry. But it's too late."

"It's not too late."

Michael grabbed the file.

"Esteemed Panel of Justices. I beg the mercy of the court to hear my father's case."

An instant hush came over the court.

"Quickly put down the file...Now!" Mr. Levy sternly demanded.

Everyone's eyes were on Michael.

"Why?"

"It is forbidden for human beings to touch anything of a Celestial nature." angrily said Mr. Levy.

"Belonging to Angels?" said Michael. "I may be a human being, and a bum at that, but I do understand some things..." Sensing that he was nearing a dangerous, even a deadly confrontation, he turned to the Justices.

"I'll put it down, Your Honors. But, please, hear my father's case."

Immediately Mr. Joseph shouted, "Don't put it down. Don't let it out of your hands. It's the only insurance you have."

A whirlwind of smoke came into the Hall, surrounded Mr. Joseph and began punishing and tormenting him.

The Hall erupted into havoc. Out of the whirlwind emanated the terrorizing and awe-inspiring VOICE OF

36

JUSTICE. "You have broken the law, Mr. Joseph. There can be no leniency", pronounced JUSTICE.

Seeing his chance to escape Michael took the file and ran into the corridor. Running for his life, he evaded the pursuing Patrol Guards hiding behind corners and blending with the background.

Unexpectedly, a hand came out from behind and covered Michael's mouth, preventing him from screaming. It was Mr. Benjamin. During the commotion in the Justice Hall he too escaped. Overpowering him, Mr. Benjamin turned Michael around and grabbed the file. Purifying it with a wave of his hand, supernatural forces flew out of the file. He began reading its documents.

"Incredible." whispered Mr. Benjamin so as not to be detected by the Patrol. "Now I understand why Mr. Joseph was adamant about your father. But why didn't the Panel of Five consider this in the first place?"

Sensing the patrol was fast approaching, Mr. Benjamin re-calibrated Michael's wristwatch.

"Listen! Winston. Something's wrong." said Mr. Benjamin. "With a file like this, your father should have never been placed in Hell Row. I set the watch to locate your father. You'll have to go into Hell Row. You have to find what your father did to get him there. I will hold off the guards."

The Patrol arrived.

"Go! Winston. You're a man. You won't be able to fight Angels. Go!"

As Michael ran away Mr. Benjamin's battling and wound-filled screams could be heard until they were heard no more, bringing Michael to a momentary pause.

He quickly took hold of himself and continued to navigate the elaborate maze of halls with the aid of the wristwatch. Each twist and turn was more terror provoking and gloomy than the previous one until he arrived into Hell Row, a place of such horror and doom that reminded him of photos of Nazi concentration camps. It was filled with countless condemned souls each wearing a black uniform and hat, slowly, hopelessly, and endlessly marching in a profound silence toward the Fires of Hell.

One soul was so distraught with fear that he collapsed and disintegrated. Only his uniform lying on the ground hinted that he was here. Seeing the uniform, Michael ran towards the condemned and pushed himself through the myriad of souls. Their footsteps had nearly shredded the uniform.

Snatching the torn garment he placed it on himself and hid among them. A live video transmission of his father marching towards the Fires appeared on the wristwatch.

# CHAPTER 7

"Pops." whispered Michael, tears rolling down his face. He scanned the marchers, spotted Jake and ran towards him. But the faster he ran, the further his father got away.

The Patrol Guards had entered Hell Row.

He pushed all the stopwatch buttons but one; and that was the transport button to take him back to earth. Still nothing helped. Out of breath, he stopped for a moment. Bending down to catch his breath, he glanced at the watch's screen and noticed that his father had stopped too. Analyzing the situation he wondered what if he walked backwards would that pull his father towards him? With each step he took backwards, Jake was pulled towards him. Walking faster and faster backwards, Jake drew closer to Michael.

Jake didn't understand why he was being pulled away from the fires.

"Come on, Pops! Start walking after me." Michael said to himself.

But Michael hadn't realized he was running towards the direction of the guards.

No matter how fast Michael walked the same distance between him and his father remained. They were like two magnets of equal strength with like charges repelled equidistantly.

Michael could hear the guards getting closer. He had to send Pops a signal.

"I'll send Pops Morse code." Michael thought to himself. As a child Jake taught Michael some of the many skills he had mastered as a combat soldier. One of those skills was Morse code.

Turning towards his father's direction he tapped out a message on the wristwatch.

'Pops. I'm here, in Hell Row. Don't worry. I'm alive.'

Jake was startled and overwhelmed to hear the message.

'Pops on my count walk towards me, no matter the resistance. Ready. One. Two. Three. Now.'

Looking at the wristwatch's monitor Michael saw Jake was confused.

Again Michael tapped out a message.

'Pops. Listen. It's me. It's me. Michael. Just start walking towards me.'

Slowly, Jake began walking towards him.

But with every step they took, the repelling forces grew, placing an incredible amount of stress on them. Determined, they struggled against the G- like Forces.

After fifteen long years, they were in sight of one another. Michael began to uncontrollably sob.

"Michael...Michael." Jake cried out, unable to contain himself.

Standing face to face they attempted to hug but were repelled by the overpowering forces.

"Pops. There isn't much time. The guards are right behind me. I tried to have a hearing but the court was stacked against you... I took your World War II file as insurance. That's why the guards are after me. They already got rid of Mr. Joseph and Mr. Benjamin."

"Fifteen years. You look good", said Jake. He was too full with emotion to listen.

"Pops. You got to focus. Mr. Benjamin said I must

40

ask you...what did you do Pops to get yourself into Hell Row?"

Jake was too ashamed to answer.

"Michael Winston. Michael Winston", called out the Patrol.

"Tell me what happened. They're coming. Tell me."

"It makes no difference", said Jake. "It's too late to change it. What is done is done... I deserve what I'm getting."

"What are you talking about? What the heck did you do?"

"Forget about it."

"No. Damn it. You haven't changed. Still the hero, for goodness' sake let me help."

"It's over. Go home. Go home."

"Go home? Go home? You're unbelievable."

"Why are you attacking me? I can't go back to the past. I can't fix the things I did wrong. You want to fix them? Mike, you don't want the burden. Just go back."

"Don't do this. Don't quit. Just tell me." Guards had arrived.

"Michael Winston. You have taken Celestial documents. You are hereby ordered to hand them over or suffer the consequences," said the commanding Patrol Officer.

"Pops. Tell me and I'll fix it."

"Give them the document. Go back."

"I'm not letting you go into Hell."

With his hand on the wristwatch he was ready to transport himself back to Earth with the Celestial documents.

The Patrol Officer noticed Mike's hand ready to

activate transport. Under no circumstances could this document be brought to Earth.

"Guards. Eliminate Mr. Winston."

As they fired their weapons Jake snatched the document as Michael pressed the transport button.

Instantly Michael was being transported back to earth while hearing Jake yelling, "Forget about me. Take care of Mommy and Danny."

# Chapter 8

Michael was now back on Earth, lying asleep near the pay phone next to Marty. He was breathing heavily, nearly out of breath, rolling in severe pain, sweating profusely, and extremely dehydrated. Fear and dread was expressed on his face. The experience in Hell Row, confronting his father, and returning to an earthly existence was overwhelming him. Desperate for air, he woke up gasping.

He crawled to Marty, grabbed onto the cart, and pulled himself up. He could hardly see. It was nearly midnight and there was poor lighting. He pushed aside the items that were on the top layer until he reached his ice chest. After living on the streets for so many years he had learned how to make his shopping cart his portable abode and home. Pulling off the ice chest lid he took out a bottle of water and gulped it down. Getting back his composure and breath, he realized his terrible predicament.

"Oh Pops! What did you do? You took the file.

What am I going to do now?"

Nervously blading back and forth, searching for a solution he recalled Uncle Leo, Jake's younger brother. Leo and Jake were extremely close since childhood. Both were athletic, handsome, fun-loving, out going, and imbued with swashbuckling personalities. They always tried emulating their favorite movie stars, Douglas Fairbanks and Errol Flynn. Everyone liked them because they were always ready and willing to help. When Jake volunteered to fight in WWII, Leo followed suit. There were inseparable, even fighting in the same unit. Who else would know more about his father than Uncle Leo? Perhaps Michael's mother, Jessica, but he was too embarrassed to approach her. He had caused her enough pain by leaving home and winding up on the streets.

With Marty in his hand, Michael skated to the nearest train towards Bayside, Queens to pay a visit to Uncle Leo.

After riding for almost an hour and rehearsing what he was going to say, Michael arrived at the Bayside Station. He hadn't seen the neighborhood in over twenty years, and Uncle Leo for fifteen years.

Blading with Marty past the single-family homes, he remembered how he dreamed of having a home and family and living in such a community. The emptiness in his soul grew wider with each home he passed.

Arriving about 100 feet from Uncle Leo's house, he removed the blades, put on sneakers, and adjusted his hair and beard. Uncle Leo hated an unkempt appearance, especially on a family member.

It was nearly two in the morning. Michael approached the door, took a deep breath, and rang the bell.

"Uncle Leo...Uncle Leo. Wake up."

Again he rang the doorbell. No answer. He walked over to the living room windows and peered through the blinds. There was no sign of Uncle Leo.

Frustrated, he walked over to Marty and removed a bullhorn.

"Uncle Leo. Wake Up...Wake Up. Uncle Leo." The surrounding neighbors turned on their lights.

Noticing the lights, Michael turned his attention to the neighbors.

"Sorry. Sorry. I forgot Uncle Leo is deaf. Well. He's

44

not really deaf. He just doesn't wear his hearing aid at night. Sorry. I forgot...everybody, just go back to sleep."

Waiting a few moments he placed the bullhorn back into the cart and walked to the rear of the house. The large tree leading to Uncle Leo's bedroom was still there. Uncle Leo always took precautions in case of a fire or burglary. The tree was his "escape ladder".

Climbing the tree, Michael's clothes got caught in the branches.

"You couldn't trim the tree in twenty years, Uncle Leo. Just a little."

Reaching the ledge he peered through the window and saw Uncle Leo. He was saddened to see that his favorite uncle had aged so much. For a moment he thought about himself and how he must have aged, which only added to his bitterness. Youth gave him the ability and hope to dream. As a middle-aged man what could he hope to achieve?

The wristwatch rang and announced.

"Five. Four. Three. Two. One. Day one has come to an end. Twenty-eight days. Twenty-three hours. Fifty-nine minutes and fifty-nine seconds remaining, Mr. Winston."

Immediately Michael snapped out from his momentary depression. There was no time to think about failure. He had to save Pops.

He tried to budge the bedroom window but it was sealed tight. Seeing he had no choice, he removed a metal bar that he kept for protection from his jacket and knocked out the window, startling Uncle Leo.

"Who the hell is there?"

"Uncle Leo, how've you been? It's me. Mike."

"Mike? Mike, who?"

"Mike. Mikey. Michael Winston...your nephew."

"What the hell is that smell?"

45

Michael hadn't taken a shower in quite some time. Uncle Leo put on his glasses and inserted his hearing aid.

"Who the hell are you?"

"Mike...Mikey."

"Mike?"

"Yeah."

"Mikey?"

He got out of bed, walked to the window, unhinged the window lock and lifted the window.

"Michael Winston. My nephew?"

He clapped his hands twice in excitement, which turned off the lights.

"Damn clap on/clap off lights. Mickey. You stink."

"Well, I've been so busy and--"

"No. You really stink. Couldn't come to your own father's funeral?!"

Upset, Uncle Leo turned his back and returned to bed.

Mike was taken aback. He never thought Uncle Leo would be angry. He always felt that Uncle Leo was too laid back to be judgmental.

Stepping into the room Michael approached him. "I need your help. It's about Pops."

"Did you visit you mother yet?"

"No, I need your help."

"Help?"

"Uncle Leo, where do you think Pop is? Metaphysically speaking?"

"Body, six feet under, but soul soaring on eagles wings upon lightening and thunder."

"Good line. That's Pops."

"I used it for the eulogy."

46

"Uncle Leo, I don't have too much time. I got to ask you a question. Did Pops ever do anything bad?"

"Boy, you really stink."

"I try. But the shower in the Y is broken. You would think after five years they would..."

"No. I mean you stink. Did Jake ever do anything bad? What kind of question is that?"

"I didn't mean it that way."

"Oh. I am sorry", he sarcastically said. "Where have you been for the last fifteen years? Couldn't call your parents once."

"Take this the right way, Uncle Leo. There's not too much time left. I got to know. Do you remember anything?Anything, when you were growing up? Anything in school? Anything later on? I got to know before it's too late. I got to know."

"Your father was a saint and hero."

Sensing that all was lost Michael broke down, sobbing.

Uncle Leo was taken aback, realizing how confused Michael was. His heart was breaking, his favorite nephew was clearly mad. Jake's passing sent him over the edge.

"It's already too late, boy."

"Don't say that. I'm not letting Pop go down into the pit."

"When was the last time you eaten?" Uncle Leo asked, wanting to comfort Michael.

"About two days ago."

"Lets' get something to eat."

"I have no time."

"You can't save your father on an empty stomach."

"You believe me?"

47

"Of course I do, Mickey. I'll get dressed and we'll go."

Deliberating the situation, Uncle Leo figured that once Michael would be in the old pub, where Jake and his cronies hung out, that would make him long for his mother. He knew that only Jessica could help him now in his time of mourning.

# Chapter 9

Shannon's Pot was an old pub that paid respect to the past while accommodating the present. Established after the War, by GI Sean O'Connor, in memory of his sister, Shannon, an army nurse stationed in the Pacific and killed in an enemy air raid, Shannon's Pot was a neighborhood fixture.

Entering the pub Michael felt uneasy, fearful he would be recognized, yet strangely hoping that he would be slightly noticed by the Old Timers, Jake's cronies, members of the infantry squad Jake led. He was moved to see the large picture of Jake in his battle uniform with a banner underneath, stating, 'A HERO FOR ALL SEASONS -THROUGH FIRE AND WATER', situated above the beer station.

The lights were low, the music soft. The pub was semi-crowded with young adults, men and women, and the Old Timers.

Jake's passing hit everyone hard, but no more so than his war buddies.

Taking their seats at a booth, Michael's stench forced the surrounding customers to move to another booth.

"You want some dessert? A piece of cake." asked Uncle Leo.

"No. I got to watch my weight."

At the Old Timers' table sat Sam, Mel, and Frank, the three other surviving commandos of Jake and Leo's battle unit. Sam was a widower, a father of four kids, a grandfather of eight grandchildren, and a retired plumber. Mel was an active real estate broker. Though a senior, he couldn't retire. His golden years had turned bittersweet. During the last ten years his beloved wife, Margret, developed Parkinson's. He was forced to work to provide for the medical expenses. And Frank never found the right one. Not because he couldn't nor wanted to get married but he just had no luck. Somehow all his luck was used up during the War to survive the onslaughts and hazards of battle. The pub became Frank's wife, and its clientele his children.

The three old soldiers stared into space, drank their beer and mourned their friend and captain. They didn't even notice Uncle Leo passing them.

Sam raised his beer glass and loudly announced, "Everyone!" getting the entire bar patrons' attention.

"A salute to Captain Jake Winston. The finest man we ever knew."

Raising their glasses, all responded in unison, "To Captain Jake Winston. The finest man we ever knew."

With beer in hand Sam walked over to Uncle Leo. "Leo...what can I say?"

"I know, Sam.Take a seat."

He sat down, gulped his beer, and turned to Michael.

"Vietnam Vet?" asked Sam, thinking that Michael was a homeless down-and-out veteran damned to live the life of the unappreciated hero.

"No. Life Vet." As the words left his lips he instantly comprehended how lost he truly was. How distant he was from ever fulfilling even one dream or ambition. He understood that he would never be the lucky few; the true artist, poet or thinker that would gift humanity with treasures of beauty, music, invention, or insight.

"Yeah...I hear that."

Turning to Uncle Leo, Sam inquired, "Did you hear from Jake's son yet?"

It was official, even the Old Timers, the men he respected the most and who knew him since he was a toddler couldn't recognize him. His shame and self-loathing seared to his core.

Uncle Leo glanced at Michael.

"No. Not yet. I'm sure he will turn up soon."

"What the hell is wrong with that boy? I hear he's living on the streets. I think between Canal and Essex...Bowery Bum Central. Incredible shame that kid. So much talent, so much waste."

"Yeah...so much talent."

"Sammy." called out Mel. "Sammy. Sammy."

"Yeah. Mel."

"Frankie says that Jake owed five grand."

"Don't be placing words in my mouth. I didn't say he owed five grand", shouted Frank.

Michael turned his attention to the Old Timers hoping that they would reveal something about Jake.

"That's you, Frank", said Mel. "You never say what you mean."

"Can I finish?"

"You couldn't say what you meant at Normandy, and you couldn't say what you meant last week when we were bowling."

For the next ten minutes Michael listened intently, but nothing but banter was spoken. Sam was about to leave the booth.

"Excuse me. Sam.", said Michael.

"Yeah." answered Sam.

"Five grand is a lot. I knew Jake Winston. He never owed that."

"You're right. Try a million, at least. Right, Leo?

51

Poor bastard."

Sam rose and returned to the Old Timers' table.

"Uncle Leo. You know something...Try a million."
Michael said sharply.

"Listen boy. Don't look at me. Ask your mother. It
concerns her."

"I got to talk to mom?"

Michael rose, walked over to the bar and looked up
at Jake's picture.

"Bartender! Give me a drink. Whiskey."

He grabbed the shot glass even before the bartender
laid it down on the counter and gulped it.

There was no turning back, Pops had to be saved. He
was going to see mom.

# Chapter 10

Pulling Marty slowly up the street leading to his parents' house, Michael noticed that his parents' bedroom was lit, though it was nearly four in the morning. Since Jake's passing it became too painful for Jessica to sleep in their bedroom. Still, every night she turned on the lights as a vigil. The lights acted as a memorial for her husband and a comfort for her. The utter darkness was too much for her to bear. She had already "lost" a son, and now she had to bear the loss of her precious husband and the love of her life.

Her only remaining pillar of strength was Danny, Michael's younger brother. Danny was a quadriplegic and mute from birth. His disabilities notwithstanding, he communicated through a computer generated voice apparatus, possessed a brilliant mind, and burned with an unquenchable passion to race. Since he was a boy Jake and Danny would race in 10k races and marathons. Jake was Danny's body. And Danny was Jake's spirit, especially after Michael left home. Jake would push Danny in a specially designed wheelchair as Danny inspired him no matter the physical hardships. There was never a race or marathon they didn't complete.

With every foot Michael took towards the house, he imagined his mom's reaction while enduring severe mental and emotional pain. His heart raced wildly, his legs and hands trembled nervously, and his mouth uttered monosyllabic groans. He was crossing inner thresholds and breaking down walls of separation. Worst of all, he was returning home after 15 years to his beloved mother, not to celebrate, but to interrogate. Facing Mom after so many years of abandonment was bad enough, but to appear out of the blue and ask her about Pops' misdeed was downright vicious, cruel and, considering her present state of mourning, might even cause her a heart attack. He had to save Pops, but at Mom's expense? He felt like a demon sent from Hell. Instantly it dawned on him that Simon might had set him up into "killing" his mom, but why? Feelings of paranoia and suspicion were suffocating him. The years of living on the streets made him mistrust everyone.

Arriving at the front door he stood motionless for the next half an hour, his body was numb, and his head was swimming. He was overwhelmed that within a flash fifteen years of self-induced exile ended, and he was home and empty-handed. Michael began sobbing, as he understood that perhaps he had been on a false and fruitless journey and search for self-discovery and art, and that all the suffering he caused to himself and to others was for nothing.

"Who's there?" said a soft voice from inside the house. It was Jessica.

Michael didn't answer.

"Who's there? I am going to call the police."

"It's ok, Jessica", said Uncle Leo.

Uncle Leo had been following Michael since he left Shannon's Pub.

"Leo?"

"Yeah, Jess."

"Who's the man standing on the porch? Where are you?"

54

"Turn on the porch light."

She turned on the light revealing Michael.

Uncle Leo stepped out from behind Michael.

Jessica opened the door.

Michael just looked at her, tears rolling down his face. He desperately wanted to hug and kiss her. Confused and helpless, Michael turned to Uncle Leo.

"Jessica. I found this guy. He says he knew Jake. Can we come in? He has some very interesting stuff to tell you about Jake."

"Let's talk on the porch. Danny has his Ph.D. oral exams tomorrow. I don't want to disturb him."

True she didn't want Danny to be disturbed, but she was also being diplomatic. She didn't want Michael's stench to enter the house.

She stepped outside, and gestured that they sit on the porch chairs.

"Ph.D. in what?" asked Michael.

"Quantum mechanics. Please sit."

Michael was stunned.

"He's a smart boy. Would you like anything to drink or eat?"

"We had something at the pub", said Uncle Leo.

"What did you want to tell me about Jake? How did you know him?"

"I'm sorry I didn't make it to the funeral. I really wanted to be there."

"That's ok. I can see that he meant a lot to you.I appreciate that very much. Where do you live?"

"Around. Where ever Marty and I can find a spot for the night."

"Marty is his shopping cart", said Uncle Leo.

"But most of the time we live at Canal Street."

Jessica's eyes lit up.

"Canal Street?! Have you ever met a man named Michael?"

Michael felt hesitant to answer; nonetheless he saw an opportunity to gently break it to Mom that he was home.

"Who is Michael?"

"My son? Years ago he left."

"What did he look like? Do you have a photo?"

Excited, Jessica raced to the house to bring one.

"Take it easy, Michael."

"I am, Uncle Leo."

Returning with the photo she held it in front of him.

"How many years ago is this photo?"

"Nearly twenty years old."

"You say he lives on Canal Street. And you haven't seen him in how many years?

"Fifteen years."

"I wonder how he would look now. I have an idea. Could you wait one minute?"

Michael rose up and walked over to Marty. Meanwhile, Jessica took her seat.

On Marty's right side Michael kept his drawing pad. He took it and returned to the porch.

"Oh. You draw. My Michael used to draw. He is a very talented boy."

"Please hold the photo in front of me", said Michael.

Michael began to draw a rendition of the photo, impressing Jessica.

"If he lives on Canal Street he probably would have long hair and a beard?" said Michael.

"Maybe?" answered Jessica slightly offended at the thought of her son being a bum.

Michael added a beard and long hair as well a shirt similar to the one he was presently wearing.

Jessica looked at it.

"What do you think?" asked Michael.

"Possible."

Michael lifted the sketch and placed it next to his face.

She saw nothing at first but as she stared at both she saw the uncanny similarities.

"Michael. Michael. Is it you Michael?

"Yeah, Ma! It's me." as he rose from his chair.

She jumped from her chair and hugged him.

"Thank God. Thank God. You brought him home, Jake.Oh! My Michael. My Michael."

"Oh! Ma. I'm sorry, Ma."

Sobbing, they embraced for nearly an hour.

The night would come to a close soon and Michael still had to confront Mom.

Composed both sat down as Uncle Leo served them tea.

"Ma. I got to ask you question."

"Yes, Baby."

"Please don't be angry."

She looked at him strangely.

"You wouldn't be angry."

"Go ahead, sweetheart."

"It's about Pops. I was talking to Sam tonight. He said something about Pops...He said that Pops owed a million, at least. I got to know, Mom. How? To who?"

"Why are you asking me this for? I am a little surprised Mikey. Why is it your concern? And why is Sam blabbing his mouth? I am getting a little upset. Fifteen years you don't show. You didn't come to the hospital. You didn't come to the funeral. And your asking question about your father? And Sam says at least a million and you couldn't shut up Sam, Leo?"

"Sam didn't realize he was talking to Mike."

"And that gave him a right to speak about such things? Because he thought he was talking to a stranger."

"Ma. It's not important that I found out. Just tell me."

Michael becomes agitated and upset.

"Come on, Mom. Just tell me. I got to know. Otherwise Pops is going into the Pit. Do you understand me? The Pit. Mr. Benjamin and Mr. Joseph told me I'm his last chance."

Mom began to realize that her precious son might be insane.

"It's ok...It's fine. Don't worry yourself. Drink some tea."

"Stop it, Ma. Stop protecting people. Always protecting. No. No. No. No. No. No."Desperate, he takes out a knife from his jacket and places it to his wrist.

"It's Malibu all over again. I can't take it anymore."

"Put down the knife. Mikey. It's not Malibu...you're upset."

"Tell me now, Ma. Now."

Twenty years earlier while Michael was living in Los Angeles he attempted suicide, thinking he was a young has-been.

"Mikey please don't...Sam meant you. You're the million reasons. You were so depressed after Malibu. You had talent and so much promise and for some reason you just couldn't make it."

"What are you saying? Pops is taking the rap for me?"

Immediately Michael shut down. It all made sense. He was his father's downfall. His father was entrusted to raise Michael and make him an upstanding and contributing member of society. Instead he was a failed man.

"It's not right. Do you hear Simon? It's not right."

Hopeless, he fell to his knees, lamenting.

Jessica was beside herself.

"I shouldn't have said a word. I am so sorry Mikey. Please, Mikey. Come into the house."

In the far off distance he noticed a fire over the horizon, reminding him of the Hell Inferno.

"I am not letting Pops go into the Pit. They want talent. I'll show them talent."

He pulled himself up, grabbed Marty and ran off.

"Mikey, come back to me", cried Jessica. "Come back."

# Chapter 11

Racing down the avenue Michael was searching for any opened Karaoke bar. Bar after bar was closing or closed until he found Jim's Karaoke Bar still open and crowded with clientele.

On stage a young man was rockin' the house with his R&B version of "Mercy".

Running into the bar, heading straight towards the stage, Michael's stench and appearance parted the crowd like the splitting of the Red Sea. About to step onto the stage, the house bouncers, Pat and Bob, grabbed and forcefully escorted him towards the entrance as he was kicking and screaming at the top of his lungs.

"Let me sing!"

Thinking quickly, Michael pretended to have a seizure. Eyes rolling backward, hands trembling, tongue curling, and mouth foaming he freaked out the bouncers.

"Hey Pat!" yelled Bob. "Bring him to the stool."

"Before he chokes to death", shouted Pat, "can someone bring a spoon for his tongue?"

Resting on the stool Michael was momentarily freed of their grip. His blood was racing with anger and determination, enraging him with fury. He knew it was the only way he could overcome the years of habitual lethargy and an iron-like mental block constantly tore at his stamina to achieve. This time he was set to unleash every talent he possessed, no matter the mental and emotional pain. Afraid of the appearance of the dreaded fog of lethargy, he immediately jumped off the stool and began to break dance to "Mercy".

The bar's owner, Jim, and the crowd's attention turned towards this homeless man spinning and jumping like a seasoned professional. At the song's end Michael, exhausted, fell to the floor to the wild cheers of the onlookers.

"How was that Simon?" said Michael.

Staggering to his feet he huffed and puffed towards the stage.

"Let me sing. Please."

The crowd began chanting, "Let him sing! Let him sing."

Sizing up the crowd's reaction, Jim instructed Pat and Bob to escort Michael to the stage.

Michael took to the stage.

Facing the audience Jim grabbed the mic.

"Very impressive dancing. What's your name?"

"Michael."

"I see you want to sing really badly. Why?"

"My father passed last week."

The crowd gasped with deep emotion.

"Is there any particular song?"

"I want to sing Pop's favorite song, Bring Him Home."

"From Les Miserables? The song about an old soldier willing to sacrifice his life to save a younger one?"

"Yeah. Pops was a World War II vet. Pops always told me to sing this song when he went. It always reminded him of his good friend's heroism. He sacrificed his life to save a younger soldier."

Jim set up the track and pressed play. All eyes were focused on this broken-hearted man anxiously waiting to hear him. Slowly the violins began. And then he sang. Instantly his beautiful and powerful tenor voice took everyone, both the ladies and the men, by surprise as he softly and tenderly sang.

"God on high he is afraid/
Let him rest/
Heaven blessed/
Bring him home/
Bring him home/
Bring him home/
He is like the son I might have known if God had granted me a son/
If die, let me die/
Bring him home/
Bring him home."

Tears rolled down the faces of the onlookers, feeling privileged to witness and participate in a bereft son lamenting his dad.

As the song ended everyone was stunned, crying, and clapping.

With mouth agape, Michael become mortified as the claps became stronger. Each validation of his performance was like a double edge sword, one side thrusting Simon's verdict, the other side thrusting Michael. For a split moment he glimpsed a life he and his family could have lived had he persevered years earlier. He now loathed himself even more imagining all the benefits he could have provided his family.

Having a near meltdown he gently returned the mic to Jim, walked off the stage and out of the pub to an ovation of cheers and slaps on the back.

Outside the pub, weeping and staggering from exhaustion, he searched for the pub's backyard for a place to lie down. Between the dumpster and the wall, he slumped to the ground and fell asleep, mumbling, "A million reasons. A million reasons."

The realization that he once had the power to help his loved ones and that he had squandered it was too great for Michael to bear. He was Orson Welles, but the later Welles, the giant that fell from grace, never to rise again. He was falling into bottomless despair.

Simon had "won". His shadow loomed and covered Michael's body and soul in the last moments of the night.

It was now up to Mr. Aaron, Mr. Levy's assistant. He was Michael's and his father's last hope.

# Chapter 12

Casually walking down the Corridor of Judgment Mr. Aaron, with hands behind his back hiding two data cards, headed towards Mission Control and entered Heaven Central.

Laid out like NASA's Cape Canaveral with supercomputers, monitors, a flat inch screen displaying a world map; the work stations were manned by a vast team of highly trained angels coordinating the countless algorithmic calculations of earthly activity as yotta trillion bytes upon yotta trillion bytes of video/audio transmissions of human interactions, both interpersonal and intrapersonal, ranging from mundane life to accidents to crimes to surviving wild weather conditions to political upheavals appeared on their terminals.

Seated at the main terminal and wearing a headset was Mr. Solomon, senior Heaven Central coordinator since the Bronze Age. A celestial of extraordinary talent and experience he was frustrated with humanity's current socioeconomic mismanagement. Displayed on his screen was an exterior shot of a downtown Manhattan tenement building burning in flames.

"Can I get a read on this?" he asked a programmer. "Look. The next backdraft needs to take place at coordinates 00.5 and 00.57...Can I have a read now? I can't activate the sequence without the read...Thank you." Receiving the coordinates he laid them in.

"Five…four...three…two…one... Activating the sequence now."

A moment later a backdraft of fire burst through the windows of the fifth floor.

Switching his monitor to an interior shot of the building, a family of four, a mother and three children, was struggling to escape to the windows, which were jammed shut.

"OK...Where are the firemen?...What? No firemen!... Code Red! Code Red!

Immediately all the angels stopped and turned their attention as the Code Red was activated.

Code Red only sounded when a human being was in an unauthorized life threatening circumstance resulting in untimely death.

"What do you mean human error? It's the fourth time this week. Not acceptable. Not acceptable. Permission to override? Thank you. Override now activated."

The jammed windows came free, enabling the family to escape to safety, to the building's ledge as the fire trucks appeared and the firemen proceeded to act.

The relieved angels applauded Mr. Solomon's action.

"Mr. Solomon. Well done", said Mr. Aaron.

"Mr. Aaron. I understand human error. I take it into account. But these people are professionals. The trucks should have been there a second earlier. I am not dealing with pre-technology humans anymore. How many times can I override the system? There is not so much leeway I have with singularity and the space-time continuum. I am tinkering with quantum structures of uncertainty."

"I understand. Mr. Solomon. We need to set up a meeting with Human Affairs. Anyhow, if you don't mind changing the subject, I have the latest information concerning the Winston case. As of now there is no verdict.

The whole hearing just fell apart."

Surprised but not wanting to press the issue Mr. Solomon nodded.

"Anyhow, I need Michael Winston's present coordinates."

Bringing up Michael on the screen he was still fast asleep behind Jim's Bar.

"Please transfer the coordinates to this card."

As he handed over the card he "accidentally" dropped it knowing that Mr. Solomon would bend to pick it up out of courtesy. Quickly Mr. Aaron slipped in the second card, which contained a loop replay of Michael sleeping.

Once the transfer was completed Mr. Solomon returned the card.

"Thank you, Mr. Solomon." "Your welcome. Mr. Aaron."

Mr. Aaron exited Heaven Central passed through the Corridor of Judgment and returned to Mr. Levy's Conference room.

Sitting at the roundtable was Mr. Levy and his closest assistants: Mr. Adam, Mr. Seth, Mr. Isaac, and Mr. Asher.

"It's done. The loop is in.", said Mr. Aaron. "Thank you", said Mr. Levy.

Quietly, he turned to the Angels of the Roundtable as he fondly called them.

"Alright. This is the first time in our five thousand years we will go against all the rules but we can't let Mr. Winston perish into oblivion. Are we all in it together? "

All nodded in agreement. "Lets' begin."

Mr. Levy passed his hand over the roundtable instantly fleshing out computers from the table's surface.

"Mr. Aaron, Mr. Isaac, please activate the coordinates."

Michael appeared on the monitor.

"Mr. Seth, Mr. Asher, commence transportation."

Risking everything, the Angels of the Roundtable stealthily sent an unauthorized Tower Light to Michael's coordinates.

Appearing and then surrounding Michael, its intensity woke him, frightening him out of his mind.

Thinking that Simon was going to kill him he desperately tried to tap the watch for help.

"They found me. Marty. Run."

Just before Mr. Solomon could detect an unauthorized transport of a terrestrial being into the celestial plane Michael was in quantum flash transport to the conference room.

But it was too late. Suspicious of Mr. Aaron, Mr. Solomon embedded a sensory algorithm while returning the card.

"Mr. Levy...Mr. Solomon outsmarted us", said Mr. Aaron. "He embedded a detector. It is a matter of moments before he realizes."

"Keeping changing the algorithms", said Mr. Levy. "We need time with Michael."

The quantum tower appeared. Out stepped Michael. "Welcome back", said Mr. Levy.

# Chapter 13

"It's you, ou backstabbing lying hypocrite lawyer!"

Michael lunged at him but was hurled backwards, burned by the celestial radiation emitting from Mr. Levy.

"Mr. Joseph and Mr. Benjamin are dead and my father is going to the Pit because of you."

"Because of me? You forgot about the million reasons? Take responsibility, Michael."

Michael stood silent.

"What am I going to do?"

"You are going to save your father."

"In twenty-eight days? Fifteen years can't be fixed in twenty-eight days."

"If you say so."

"What do you mean if I say so?!"

Mr. Levy signaled Mr. Adam to activate a massive theatrical screen to appear on the wall.

Fading in on the screen was a beautiful shot of the Rhine River on a dark overcast late afternoon. Panning from left to right, a war torn ruin came into view as a fierce exchange of combat fire intensified the battlefield's dread. Tracking in a smooth yet dramatic manner the camera captured the figures of ten American GIs, led by a charismatic, highly kinetic, take-charge squad leader, as they were taking cover in the ruin from German enemy fire.

Awestruck by the sheer mastery of the camera work and editing, Michael was mesmerized. Never had he witnessed such craft, artistic expression, and virtuosity.

"This is incredible. Who shot this?" "Mr. Asher and Mr. Adam."

"This is breathtaking, fellas. What camerawork! Incredible actors!"

Mr. Levy motioned Mr. Adam to zoom into the frame.

"Hey, who is that in the background? It's Pops! This is real. Wow!...Freeze frame."

Mr. Adam froze the action.

Michael walked towards the screen, his eyes fixed on his young father, he stood silently, taking immense pride in the dashing and heroic figure Pops cut, commanding his squad and bravely fighting the enemy.

"All my life I wanted to see Pops in action."

"It's the fellas. I can't believe it. Uncle Leo, Mel, Frank, Sam. They were all so young. This is fantastic! Is this the WWII file?"

"Yes", said Mr. Levy, "This is the Light Transmission of March 7, 1945, Battle of Regamen near the Rhine River. Since the moment "Let There Be Light" was first uttered Light Transmissions have been used both to record and transmit information across the entire space-time continuum. Mr. Adam and Mr. Asher are our top war photographers and camera angels."

"Who are the other five GIs?"

"Jack, Billy, Otis, Tommy and Phil. Very nice guys."

"Please play the footage", said Michael.

Continuing the transmission, the Germans were steadily advancing.

"Capt.", yelled Phil.

"Yeah. Phi,l" responded Jake.

"There's three German tanks coming at us."

Imitating Scarlet O'Hara, Leo sarcastically asked, "A

German tank. A German tank! But what ever shall we do, Captain?"

"Well, Scarlett", answered Jake, imitating Clark Gable, "Why, blow it up my dear."

"But how? We're all out of shells", continuing as Scarlett.

"Otis!" yelled Jake.

"Yeah, Capt."

"How far is the cliff?"

"About one thousand feet."

"All right, fellas. On the count of three everyone head towards the cliff. Once we are there we'll knock out the tank from the rear...OK...One...Two...Three..."

A tank shell hit, collapsing the walls and trapping all of them, except for Jake.

Badly shaken, Jake surveyed the damage. There was rubble everywhere.

"Leo! Leo! Sam! Mel! Anybody!" shouted Jake.

"I'm ok, Jake", said Sam.

"Me too", replied Mel.

"Hold on fellas."

"Save yourself before the Germans get here, Jake", yelled Frank.

"Shut up, Frank. Nobody dies on my watch."
"Where is Leo?" yelled Jake.

With every bit of his strength he began to dig Sam, then Mel and then Frank out of the rubble.

"Come on, fellas. Before the Krauts arrive. Help me."

All four then pulled out Jake, Otis, Phil, Billy, and Tommy in succession. All were badly injured.

Another enemy shell hit, catching the ruin on flames. "We are sitting ducks!" yelled Sam.

A downpour began, which slowed down the

Germans but hindered Leo's rescue.

"Jake! Jake!" shouted Leo.

"Leo! Leo! Where are you?"

"Jake! He's over there," yelled Sam.

The flames were engulfing the area surrounding Leo.

"I am coming, Leo. Hold on."

Jake attempted to run into the fire but was pushed back by the flames.

"Damn it! Damn it!"

He jumped on the ground and rolled on the earth, trying to place as much dirt as he could on his clothes.

"It's not enough. I need more earth."

Quickly the fellas dug up earth and covered him. Standing up, he adjusted his gear.

"Your face!" said Mel. "The flames."

Jake removed his helmet, took his revolver and shot three holes making openings for his eyes and nose and then covered his face with it.

"What are you, nuts, Jake?" shouted Frank. "You'll burn your face off from the helmet's metal."

Leo was now screaming as the flames licked his body. "Give me your jacket!" said Jake.

Frank handed it over.

"Hold it tight."

Jake took his knife, cut holes in the jacket, covered his face and placed the helmet on.

"I am coming little brother! To Victory!"

He jumped into the flames.

Both were screaming as the flames overcame them.

The transmission suddenly ended, closing the file, and swallowing up the screen.

"What the hell? What happened?" said a stunned Michael.

"That's not the whole file. The rest can't be opened", said Mr. Levy.

"You're kidding me. So use this. At least show this segment to the court. Pops is a hero for jumping in."

"We can't show the court for the same reason we can't open the whole file."

Michael was puzzled.

"You still don't understand…for a million reasons Michael... Fathers and sons....The file can't be open until you right your life. You right your life, your right your father's life...It's all about fathers and sons."

"What do I need to do?"

"Get cleaned up. Get a job. Harness your talents. Get married."

"What? Get married?! And all of these in twenty-eight days?!"

Michael's head began spinning with anxiety. Feeling faint he fell backwards into a deep wormhole of time-space hearing Mr. Levy's words echo, "Don't fail your father."

Arriving back in the backyard of Jim's Bar Michael woke up and sprang to his feet. Determination was burning in his soul. For the first time in over twenty years he felt alive again. He had a purpose.

Grabbing Marty, he started running down the dawn lit street yelling, "To Victory!"

# Chapter 14

Nearing the Local Y, The Homeless Shelter for Men, Michael ran to the foot of the building and secured Marty in the allocated shopping cart lot, marked, "SHOPPING CARTS ONLY. VALET PARKING EXTRA." He entered the dimly lit hall filled with hundreds of homeless men sleeping on cots and ran towards the shower room, accidentally brushing against Wild Bill's bed.

"What the hell?" said a half-asleep Wild Bill.

A moment later, water was heard running in the shower room, shocking Wild Bill. Opening one eye and then another he turned to the shower room and saw Michael holding a bar of soap in one hand and a pair of scissors in the other. Michael removed his clothing and stepped into the shower letting out a wild scream.

Wild Bill ran around the hall waking everyone shouting, "Mickey lost it!"

As the shower ended a large crowd formed outside waiting to see Michael.

Stepping out of the shower room in his shabby clothes and torn shoes was a cleaned-up, clean shaved and handsome man.

All were in shock.

Leaning against the wall he gathered his energy and breath. The experience had exhausted him. It was the first shower he took in nearly fifteen years.

"Everyone stand back. Mikey is having a breakdown," said Wild Bill. "Just take it easy, Mikey.

You need 911."

"No. Just some pain killers."

Letting out a scream, he braced himself like a fighter ready for the next round and burst forth towards the hallway and to the exit as the residents stood flabbergasted.

Running down the avenue with Marty, Michael caught sight of a "Help Wanted" sign on a shoe store window. Crossing the heavily laden traffic, car horns were blasted at him.

"I'll take the job," screamed Michael. "I am good with shoes. I have worn them all my life."

Peering out the storefront window, the manager was frightened at this disturbing sight. As Michael was about to step onto the sidewalk the manager removed the sign.

"Oh. Come on, I got my own shoe horn. Alright. Marty. Forget this heel. Next."

Sprinting down the avenue, he spotted another "Help Wanted" sign hanging in a pet store display. He pulled out a bullhorn from the cart and blared.

"I love gerbils and hamsters. I support animal rights."

As he neared the shop, the startled storeowner waved his arms gesturing the job was unavailable.

"What the...I am not an animal.I am a human being."

"You see that, Marty? It's the Elephant Man all over again."

Turning his head, he saw another "Help Wanted" sign swinging from the overhang of Willcombs' camera rental store. "Cameras! Marty! Cameras! Yahoo! Come on! Our luck is changing."

Michael charged ahead. He ran into Willcombs, leaving Marty by the door.

Willcombs was a large store filled with lighting kits,

Boolex and Arrri 16 mm cameras, various dv and digital camcorders, avid editing equipment and accessories. A fixture of the neighborhood, its owners, college buddies, Wayne, and Ross had turned it into a film enthusiast cove.

"I'll take the job. I'll take the job."

"Hi. What's your name?" asked Ross.

"Michael."

"I'm Ross.

"I got the job? When can I start?"

"Do you have any training?"

"NYU. New School. NYFA. I have worked with Charlie Gates."

"You're kidding me. Charlie Gates. Hey! Wayne! He says he's worked with Charlie Gates."

"Cool", said Wayne.

Both didn't believe him, but neither wanted to offend.

"Well. Do I get the job?"

"Everything sounds good. Hate to put you on the spot. But do you have a resume?"

"What about my diplomas? I have them outside."

"Diplomas are fine. But we need to see your work? Do you have any photos, videos, or film samples? Or a reel of your work?"

"I do...But everything is in Queens at home."

"That's fine...go to Queens...go home and bring it to us. We will be here."

"You're not playing with me."

"Not playing. If you got the goods, we will hire you."

"Alright Man .Be back in two hours . Later."

"Later." said Wayne and Ross.

Excited Michael ran out. "Marty. We got a job. "He kissed Marty and took off to Queens.

Halfway down the block the stopwatch received a text, "EMERGENCY! FIND A PAY PHONE NOW! IT'S ME, MR. LEVY."

"Oh, no! What happened now?"

Searching for over ten blocks, he found one.

"Marty, why do they always have to use pay phones? They need to work out a deal with the phone company. I don't know, Marty. May be celestials aren't allowed to buy a phone plan? No budget for that. That's a good one, Mart You are getting funnier. You're welcome."

Nearly a half an hour passed and no call.

"Marty. I don't like this. Something is not good. Don't tell me to calm down. Again with the positive thinking speech. I promised Wayne and Ross I would be back in two hours. You can't say--"

The phone rang. Immediately Michael answered.

"What is wrong now? I got a job interview. They aren't going to hire me if I am late."

"Michael", Mr. Levy said in a serious tone.

"What?"

"I have some very sad news. The file is gone."

"What do you mean? Gone? How?"

"The Counsel and I weren't certain if you were going to pull off the--"

"What? I got cleaned up. I'm about to be hired."

"We might be angels but we can't see the future regarding human actions. You were a gamble."

"What did you do?"

"We attempted a raid-like mission into Hell Row."

"A commando-like raid into Hell Row? Since when did you guys become CIA? I don't believe this."

"Somehow Simon found out. He intercepted us and kidnapped your father."

"What?!?"

76

"And..."

"And what else?"

"The file...Simon destroyed it."

"Oh, no! You killed my father. You killed him. Without the file, it's over."

Shocked, he slowly hung up the phone hearing Mr. Levy remorsefully say, "I am so sorry, Michael."

Falling against Marty, he thundered a death scream.

"It's over Marty."

The phone rang again. Barely able to lift his arm he answered it.

"What do you want to tell me now?"

"Is that anyway to talk?" said Simon. "Don't think your mission is over. Just the stakes are higher now. Can't wait to see Danny." A text message arrived on Michael's watch. "Read the text I just sent!"

The message read, 'Queensborough Bridge. Bring flowers for Danny.'

"Leave my brother out of this, you son of--"

Dial tone.

Michael took a quarter and dialed home.

"Ma. It's me. Where is Danny...Where is he? ...At the campus...Which one? ...He just texted you...Is he on his way home?...ok...Text him not to take the Queensborough...Please Ma. Just do it...What do you mean your phone battery died.... I'll talk to you later."

Michael hung up the phone.

"That's it. Nobody touches my little brother. Come on, Marty!" Michael took off towards the bridge.

# Chapter 15

Approaching Queensborough, Michael was furiously searching for an Ambulette transport vehicle that was Manhattan bound. Nearly three quarters across the bridge he spotted a halted Ambulette with its side door open and three figures outside the vehicle.

He took out a pair of binoculars from the cart to get a better look. It was Danny and his two attendants, Patrick and Robert. Both were frantically trying to save Danny. He was convulsing and choking to death on his own saliva. Unable to open his mouth they lifted him out of the wheelchair, however, due to his inability to stand they held his body in mid-air and administrated the Heimlich maneuver, but to no avail. Simon had cleverly made the Heimlich useless by having Danny choke on his own saliva.

Michael pulled out the bullhorn and yelled above the traffic sounds.

"Danny! Danny! Listen to me. It's Mickey."

Danny's eyes lit up for a moment.

"Focus on the race. Thorpize it...Thorpize it!"

As a kid the Native American athlete Jim Thorpe fascinated Danny, proclaimed the world's greatest athlete in the 1912 Stockholm Olympic Games. Thorpe possessed the remarkable ability to visualize his races. While others trained on the voyage ship bound to the Games, Thorpe lay on his cabin bed and visualized his every stride, turn, jump, and shot put needed for the Decathlon. His "training" resulted in a legendary athletic performance.

"Thorpize it" was the term Danny coined for the method. Whenever Pops hit the "wall of pain" during their races he would cheer him on, chanting, "Focus on the race, Thorpize it".

"Come on Danny. Thorpize.", yelled Michael.

Danny closed his eyes, slowed down his heartbeat and "Thorpized" his throat muscles relaxing. Within moments the choking stopped. When Danny opened his eyes Michael was standing before him.

"Hi, Little brother."

Michael hugged and kissed him.

Danny was not happy to see Michael resentful of his abandonment fifteen years earlier.

Michael introduced himself to Patrick and Robert. They then sat Danny in his wheelchair and reconnected his voice apparatus.

"Mickey. Who is Simon?", asked Danny.

"You saw Simon?"

"What are we going to do? He took Pops, then he tried to get me. Who's next? Mom? What does this guy want?" asked Danny.

"He told you about Pops? Lets get you back into the van. We need a quiet place to talk."

"Robert, please take me to my office.", asked Danny.

As Patrick and Robert were placing Danny back into the Ambulette Michael secured Marty to its back bumper.

En route now to Danny's office at the university a massive rainstorm began. Or so it seemed. While the other vehicles were driving in normal weather conditions the time-space continuum for Michael, Danny, and the attendants had detached itself from reality. To them all the vehicles on the roadway were in a rainstorm. To anyone who was observing the Ambulette it was driving in normal weather conditions.

"It's too dangerous to drive.", said Robert.

"Lets pull over.", Patrick said. "Danny. I am going to sit in the front with Robert while we wait for the rain to stop. You and your brother can have some privacy to talk."

Patrick moved up forward and sat in the passenger's seat.

"Tell me about--" said Danny.

"Yes. Mikey. Tell him," announced Simon's unexpected voice.

"What the--", shouted Michael.

"The Hell," quipped Simon.

Simon had entered the Ambulette and proceeded to wrench out Danny's soul.

"Mickey. Help me!" said Danny.

Mr. Levy's halogen image appeared.

"Your watch. Michael. Point it to the east.", said Mr. Levy.

Michael lifted his wrist and pointed it towards the east. A cone-like ray of bright light descended and enveloped Danny.

Danny's inner essence left his body. For the first time in his life he was free to move, walk, smile, and talk.

"Oh my God! You can move. Danny. You can move.", Michael joyously shouted.

"What did you do Levy?" yelled Simon.

Freeing Danny's inner essence hindered Simon from removing Danny's soul.

"I can move!" shouted Danny.

"You can talk, Danny!", said Michael.

Michael was crying uncontrollably seeing his little brother talking and walking. It was a dream come true.

"Simon.", said Mr. Levy. "You're in breach of every code. 28 days...The court ruled that Mr. Winston has 28 days to complete the tasks and you have interfered."

"I interfered? You attempted a raid.", responded Simon.

"This is lawlessness. Danny move towards Simon.", said Mr. Levy.

Simon backed away, afraid to come into contact with Danny. Now that his inner essence was set free while still alive he was a celestial human being that even Simon needed protection from.

"Fine. Mr. Levy. But Michael's tasks are no longer."

"Then I offer you the Race.", said Mr. Levy

"Not the Race.", said Simon.

"Why worry?", stated Mr. Levy.

"But you are including Danny Winston," said Simon.

"I am also referring to Michael Winston. So what do you have to lose? He's not exactly the embodiment of mental health, stability, and discipline.", answered Mr. Levy.

Michael's arm was becoming tired, making it difficult for him to maintain the wristwatch towards the East, causing the cone light to move away from Danny, effecting Danny's ability to move freely.

"Both Winston's...Are you serious?" asked Simon.

"Dead serious." responded Mr. Levy.

"Three for the price of one. I can get all three Winston's", thought Simon.

Exhausted, Michael dropped his arm. Immediately Danny's inner essence fell back into his paralyzed body.

"Michael. How could you? Letting your brother

81

return to that prison of a body.

"Shut up. You bastard."

"Agreed." laughed Simon. "Three for the price of one."

A moment later Simon left.

"Well, gentlemen." said Mr. Levy.

"What race?" Asked Danny.

"The one you and your Father always dreamed of entering."

"No way!", said Danny. "There is no way in hell Mikey can get in shape for the triathlon in three weeks. Even Pops could not do it."

"Triathlon? Competition...with people...oh no. I don't compete," said Michael.

"This is our last card." Simon agreed. "You do this and the court will reverse its decision."

"What if I lose?"

"Just like that? Giving up already? Oh, Mikey," said Danny.

"Hey. I don't compete...ok...I don't do competition...ok...just leave me alone. People watching me, judging me. Do it this way, Mike. Do it that way, Mike...I am surprised at you, Mike. I thought you could do it, Mike...But you are so talented, Mike....Let them try...Let them see how it feels....It's Malibu all over again. Malibu...Malibu...Malibu...It never ends...everyone staring...everyone looking..."

"Don't think about it...Just focus...", said Mr. Levy.

"Don't think about it...just like that...I don't do competitions."

"Fifteen years...uh man...fifteen years and still the same...", said Danny, "Mr. Levy. Forget Mike. If the race is what it takes I'll get someone else."

"Simon won't agree to that. It's both of you or none

82

of you.", said Mr. Levy.

"Don't think about it...", said Michael, "Yeah right...Who's going to train me?"

"Your brother."

"In three weeks...what does the triathlon entail?"

"A fifty mile bicycling tour over rough terrain, a thirteen-mile swimming event, and a twenty-six mile marathon. All in three days."

"Are you nuts?...And what is Danny going to do?"

"You're going to be pulling him."

"Pulling him?...This is crazy...What am I? His father?"

"No. His older brother...Think about it...Do you realize how well-trained you are for this?....You have been pushing Marty all these years...excuse us Danny...I need to speak to Michael alone."

Mr. Levy blocked Danny's hearing.

"What's wrong with you? For the past several days you have demonstrated to the court impressive--"

"But--"

"Don't interrupt me. You have demonstrated very impressive traits and qualities...You are so close Michael...so close…don't fail. Bad enough you ruined your past. Don't ruin your father's future. Do you understand me, Michael? The dead have no choice. No opportunity to change the future. Only the living...I don't know what's going to happen. Win or lose, you must race. If your father is going to the Pit forever at least give him something to hold onto...Is that clear?"

"Clear...I love my father."

"Good." Mr. Levy unblocked Danny's hearing. "Well, boys. Good luck. Bye."

Mr. Levy's halogen transmission ended.

Michael was breathing heavily out of fear and

agitation, contemplating the enormous challenge ahead.

Pacing back and forth he visualized Pops' end.

""Marty...What do you think?...Fail once, shame on you. Fail twice, shame on me...Yeah Marty..."

Michael and Danny stared into each other's eyes with great intensity.

"Thorpize it?" asked Michael.

"Thorpize it." replied Danny.

"Son of a...Lets do it!" Exclaimed Michael.

# Chapter 16

"I got it!" Shouted Michael. "Brothers run triathlon to honor late father."

The preparations, planning, and a training schedule were underway but when Simon said, "Michael's tasks were no longer" he meant Michael still had to meet his earlier tasks along with The Race. Together Danny and Michael brainstormed various means to meet the tasks.

"I need to harness my talents. Right? I'll make a video movie blog. I'll shoot in a cinematic style. I'll use two cameras, one on you and the other on me. This way we will get both points of view."

Though Michael had been living on the streets he was abreast of all the latest technology. The challenges were activating his latent genius. Even Danny postponed his PH.D oral examinations for the following semester. Nothing was going to stop them.

"Yes. We'll place daily episodes on all the social media and blog outlets", added Danny.

"Great marketing", said Michael. "And we mention that I need to find a wife otherwise our late father won't rest in peace." "I'm telling you this sounds so weird and cool that people will be glued to their PCs and phones."

The plan was set: a web series about the race to harness his talents, social media and blog outlets to bring recognition leading to employment, publicizing his quest for a wife to get married, and training for The Race.

Training from home, Jessica would sit for hours

watching, "drinking in" the time lost and now found. With every stare, her empty soul was filling up. From time to time she would cry uncontrollably, just thankful to see her Michael home again.

During the first three days of training Michael was physically strong, but, mentally, bouts of fear and anxiety would overwhelm him. Michael bicycled; pulling Danny in the specially designed wheelchair Pops had constructed years earlier. His over-demanding expectations to have the perfect shot for the video blog resulted in bursts of anger, yelling, and moments of insanity.

"What the hell are you doing?" said Uncle Leo. "Just take the damn video.This is not Citizen Kane."

"Yeah. Everything is Citizen Kane", answered Michael.

"I have no idea why both of you are training for this race. You are a middle-aged man acting like a teenager", said Uncle Leo.

"You want to know why? I'll tell you when you tell me what happened when Pops jumped in after you in that burning building at the Battle of Regamen", said Michael.

"Who told you?" asked Uncle Leo. Uncle Leo gave Michael a cold stare, looked away in shame and walked.

"That's right Uncle Leo. Iam not the only one with something burning in my soul, tearing me apart like a backscatter machine gun. Either help me or back off."

Uncle Leo turned back to Michael.

"Who told you anything about that battle?", asked Uncle Leo.

Michael realized he spoke too much.

"Who told you?"

"I asked who told you? Was it Simon?"

Michael's expression confirmed his suspicions.

"I knew that son of a weasel would be back."

Uncle Leo took both hands, grabbed his buttoned shirt placket, ripped open the shirt and pointed to Simon's handprint seared into his flesh. For over seventy years he had carried Simon's mark on his chest.

"This is what Simon left me with at the Battle of Regamen."

"What does he want with you and Danny?"

Michael and Danny told him the whole story.

"Alright, boys! Whatever the reason this son of a weasel has in against the Winston family let's send this bastard back to Hell...The training will be under my direction. It's 82nd airborne all the way."

Uncle Leo organized the training with the help of Sam, Frank, and Mel. Neither Jake nor Leo ever told them what happened in the fire. They were afraid any information would endanger their friends. Apprehensive with Simon's return Leo took comfort that both he and Jake had the wisdom to keep the incident hidden from them. The only reason he gave the fellas entrance into Michael's and Danny's Race was because they wanted to honor Jake. And that was all they needed to know "to take the hill". They were the 82nd, the underdog that no one betted on, but always, against all odds, got the job done. For the next twenty-five days nothing existed for them but to train Michael and Danny to achieve victory to honor their Captain. The Old Timers' great athletic knowledge and grit was on fire.

They turned Jessica's backyard into a boot camp with ropes to climb, tires to run through, and weights to lift. In the morning they rode alongside Michael as he pushed Danny across the service roads. In the afternoon they took him to the Rockaways to swim in the ocean and pull Danny.

Each day a new video blog was posted, drawing more viewers to the PR sensation Michael and Danny were creating. Within a week Michael's masterful videos with music, sound, and dialogue went viral. News channels were taking notice of "The Two Brothers Training for a Race to Honor Their Late Father". A broken down homeless man and a quadriplegic/mute dedicating themselves to honor their late father, a WW II hero became the topic on everyone's mind.

Day by day, all types were becoming attached to their quest: adult home residents, sick children in hospitals, senior citizens, war vets, school children, the homeless, down and out men and women, and even bankers on Wall Street. They were touching a chord within people. Two sons, against all odds, attempting to honor their beloved father through trial and tribulation, is heroic and inspiring. People were stunned to see what gratitude looked like, and how two sons were paying back their father for his great devotion and love he had shown them.

The strategy was working. Michael was receiving job offers for his poignant videos and even marketing agencies were taking notice of his PR savvy.

One particular agency, Johnson and Briggs, was especially interested in Michael's quest to find a wife. During the past six months the agency was building a marketing campaign for their recent client, Marrymenow.com. Seeing the public's fascination with Michael the agency thought it would be great to use Michael's quest as a marketing ploy for their client. It was decided that their top marketing agent would receive the assignment. Though the agent had been out of the office preparing for her wedding what better person could get insight and create a marriage campaign. Her upcoming nuptials and Michael's quest would enable her supple mind to market Marrymenow.com in an exciting manner.

Late at night, attending to her email, she received the information about the Race. Reviewing the material she realized the homeless man was the one that saved her from the speeding train two weeks earlier. As she stared at the photos of this homeless man she was shocked and dumbfounded.

"My God! It's Michael.", said Lisa Hoffman. She had long given up hope of ever seeing the love of her life.

Within twenty-three days she was going to marry, and somehow, from nowhere, Michael was back in her life.

She sobbed throughout the night. The man she loved more than her own life was back but it was too late.

# Chapter 17

Morning had arrived and Lisa was barely able to get off the floor. She spent years attempting to forget Michael. It was not because he was bad to her. He had a heart of gold. But the temperament of an artist and the fear he had as a failed man drove a wedge between them. No matter how she tried to uplift him and be his helpmate he pushed her away. And when finally he could accept her help it was too late, her heart had been broken too often.

But of all the suffering she had endured, none compared as to find a wife for the love of her life. She cursed the day she was born. Slowly she got dressed, put on her makeup, took her handbag and laptop, exited her apartment, locked the door, and left the building. Each movement felt like a ton.

She wanted to scream. About to enter the subway station, she immediately turned and ran to the closest cafe. She needed noise, the sound of people to distract the pain. She decided to work from the cafe and took out her laptop. But it was useless. Everyone, or it seemed like everyone, was talking about the Winston Brothers. It was maddening.

Lisa began working on Marrymenow.com campaign. Playing one of Michael's video blogs, Lisa saw herself in a montage he had made of his favorite people. Throughout all the years Michael was on the streets, a worn out photo of Lisa gave him the strength to pass each day. Transfixed on the montage Lisa felt it was retribution, as if the hand of fate was punishing her for not going the extra mile, otherwise why else would Michael come back into her life just before her wedding. She felt her punishment was to find a wife for Michael. If she was not going to be alone, neither could he.

As the day transpired her torment increased in intensity. Slowly, old feelings were reawakening again. She was starting to question her feelings for her fiancé. She loved him. He was good, stable, protective, and even a romantic man. She had to get away from Michael. But of course she couldn't. The agency needed the campaign and she needed to pluck Michael out of her soul. She emailed Michael about her agency, the Marrymenow.com PR campaign and how both could help find him a wife, but she used an alias, Mary Bailey, the character from *It's A Wonderful Life*. She always felt like the young Mary, a girl and then a young woman attached to her man but never appreciated by him, until years later. Michael was excited that a Manhattan PR agency was taking on his quest.

Within hours after Lisa placed a blog ad for Marrymenow.com and Michael's search, women were posting their photos and resumes on it. Many even attended Michael and Danny's training sessions. Some of them were sincere, others wanted to be part of the adrenaline rush of a quest, and others just wanted their fifteen minutes of fame. But Lisa was clever, and slightly jealous. She had designed a questionnaire to weed out all the flakes and scams. But as the days passed Michael took notice of the low number of women that were eligible. Each time he sent an email to Lisa - Mary - he always got the runaround why the process was taking so long.

It was now eight hours before the race, and still Michael had no wife. Lying in bed in his room and "Thorpizing" the Race in his mind, it suddenly occurred to him that perhaps the agency was prolonging the search to bring more traffic to Marrymenow.com. His worst fears were confirmed when he spoke to Dan Green, Vice President of the agency and learned that Mary Bailey didn't exist, but rather Lisa Hoffman was running the campaign. Michael was burning with anger and hurt to discover that Lisa was behind the campaign. He was angry because Lisa had lied to him; upset, because he felt manipulated; and devastated because she did not reach out to him. All these years he hoped she still loved him. To learn she didn't, and the fact that he was just being used as a marketing tool was a crushing blow. Within minutes he was pacing wildly, throwing objects, and yelling wildly.

Jessica, Uncle Leo, and Danny rushed to his room.

"What a lowlife, two timing, little... Ma...I just can't take it," Michael shouted. "There is no Mary Bailey. Lisa Hoffman is behind the Marrymenow.com campaign. Can you imagine, Lisa Hoffman? How could she do this to me? Vengeful, backstabbing...."

"Stop it!", said Mom. "First of all, how do you know it is the same Lisa Hoffman? And second of all, do you recall you abandoned her?"

"Are you taking her side? Her side. I didn't abandon her. I was having a nervous breakdown. She left me", said Michael.

"After you told her to leave", responded Mom.

"I didn't mean it", said Michael

"You broke her heart", replied Mom.

"Well, if she really loved me she should have gone the extra mile", demanded Michael.

Michael then received a text message from Simon.

"You have done well, Mr. Winston. Surprisingly. Cleaned up. Harnessed Talent. Got a job. Impressive. But no wife! Oh. I forgot to tell you, none of the women are permitted to marry you. Those are the rules. Let me rephrase myself. None of the women are permitted to you to marry but one, Lisa Hoffman. Remember her? And she is getting married within three days. Just at the end of the Race...Check mate!"

Michael fell back, nearly fainting. His worst fear came true Lisa was lost to him. He fell into a deep depression. Within three days he would lose both his beloved father and the love of his life.

Uncle Leo saw the text.

"Simon!" yelled Uncle Leo. "The boy has done everything. You have to give him something!"

Jessica was at a loss to what was occurring.

Another text message appeared.

"Confront Lisa face-to-face."

Uncle Leo picked up Michael and placed him on the bed.

"Come on, boy. You need to save Pops. Don't give up the fight."

Lisa was the last person he wanted to meet.

"Meet the woman. You have no choice. But don't be emotional. Simon wants to set you up. The past is the past. What you and her had years ago leave it there."

The phone rang.

Jessica answered it.

"It's for you, Michael. It's someone named Simon", said Mom.

Michael took the phone.

"Well, Mr. Winston. The Night Tribulations begin. Just you. Don't take Marty. Next phone call Queens Blvd and Union Turnpike. Go."

Dial tone.

Michael looked at Uncle Leo and Danny.

"I'm going. Give me a kiss Ma. I'll be back in time for the Race. I am not letting you down this time."

Michael exited and took off running.

Night had ended as the sun was appearing over the Manhattan skyline and still Michael Winston was no closer to saving Jake. Throughout the harrowing night he was manipulated into running fifty blocks desperately racing from ringing pay phone to pay phone, answering the calls on time, fulfilling the sadistic demands of Simon. He taunted and played with him like a mouse caught in a trap. With his lungs burning from exhaustion he managed to answer another one.

"How many times do I have to tell you? This is not a game", said Simon.

"What do you think I am doing? Fooling around? I am doing my best", pleaded Michael.

"Your best", retorted Simon, "Tell that to your father when      we      send      him      to      hell."
"Let me talk to my father", yelled Michael. "Let me--"

Simon hung up leaving Michael with only the dial tone.

Frustrated, Michael banged the receiver.

"Please. Please."

From the side of his eye he noticed a homeless man walking up the sidewalk, pushing a shopping cart. "Sid. Sid", shouted Michael.

"Who wants to know?"

Unfamiliar with Michael's cleaned up and well-dressed look Sid couldn't recognize him.

"It's me. Mike. Michael. Mikey."

"Mikey? What happened to you?"

94

"They got my father! They're going to take him down."

Off in the distance another pay phone was ringing.

"You got to help me, Sid. You got to." Michael reached into his right hand jacket pocket removed a digital recorder and handed it over to him.

Another pay phone rang, chiming in harmony with the first phone. "It's all here. I got to go."

"Lisa lives at 545 Park Avenue. Apartment 3F", said Simon. "Confront her now."

Simon had tired Michael out. The confrontation was set. Within a few moments, they would break any connection they had and victory would go to Simon, and Jake would be done and lost in the Pit forever.

# Chapter 18

Michael arrived in front of the building. He knew Lisa would not allow the doorman to let him enter if he announced his name. To outmaneuver her he told the doorman that her boss, Dan Green, had sent a hand delivered package via courier that had to be taken personally and could not be left at the desk. Half asleep, she came downstairs wearing a sweatshirt over her nightgown, no makeup, and hair uncombed.

Focused, upset, and seething with anger, Michael waited in the lobby and took note of the floor number the elevator stopped, eighteen. Michael lowered his head down to hide his face as Lisa stepped out of the elevator.

"Good morning", said Lisa. "Where is the item please?"

As she put her hand out, Michael placed the worn photo of her in it.

"Oh, my God!" She said, startled by the photo.

She looked up, locked eyes with Michael's burning eyes and stood with mouth agape, as if she had her life punched out of her. Her heart was racing wildly. She could not feel her footing. She dropped the photo.

Michael picked it up.

"How's it going, Mary?" said Michael.

They gazed into each other's eyes. Both were full of pain, anguish, longing, resentment, and deep hurt. They stood face-to-face in silence. Nearly two minutes passed.

She pulled him aside. Michael jerked his arm back.

Lisa pointed towards the mailroom, gesturing they go there for privacy.

Alone in the mailroom, he stood and just stared into her eyes recalling his suffering and abandonment.

"What is it, Michael?"

"Fifteen years, Mary."

"Don't call me Mary. And by the way, you are no George Bailey."

No matter how difficult or interfering things got in his life, George Bailey always did the right thing and placed others before his needs.

"That's right. And this ain't no wonderful life. Still comparing me to George Bailey. Well in that case, I didn't do too badly when I saved you from the oncoming train."

"You see, you saved me and then you left me. Nothing has changed."

"Are you kidding me? Now you are complaining about that too."

"I am not complaining. Oh, I don't know what I am saying. I am very grateful to you. It was very heroic of you. Just like your father. I just wanted to thank you...to talk to you."

"Did you know it was me?"

"No. Why did you leave so suddenly?"

"I didn't want you see me as a bum, a broken down man. That's why I left. Why did you lead me on with the marrymenow.com campaign?"

"I didn't mean to. My boss forced me to take the assignment."

"Yeah. I figured that. But why did you manipulate the search? Are you still so selfish? You're getting married in three days anyhow and I have to be condemned to walk the earth alone. You couldn't even help me find someone", said Michael.

"Who told you about my wedding?...I didn't mean to do any wrong to you." Said Lisa.

"But you did. Fifteen years Lisa. Fifteen years I dreamed about you. Longed for you", said Michael.

"And what about me? What about me? I waited for you. I cried for you. Michael Winston, failed genius. Michael the genius, too scared to fight for the woman he loved. I was yours, Michael. Yours for the taking."

"Do you love him?"

"Of course."

"Do you love him like you loved me?"

"What kind of question is that? For a genius you sure are an idiot. And you are no gentleman either. Coming to my home without warning me. How could you not give a girl a chance to make herself up?"

"Well, do you love him like you loved me?"

"Leave me alone Michael."

She quickly left the mailroom and headed to the elevator.

"And by the way, I did try to find you a wife. But you know what? Nobody is good enough for you. You're a blood sucker", said Lisa. "No...Let me correct myself...a soul sucker."

The elevator arrived.

Michael was stunned.

Lisa stepped into the elevator.

"Good luck in your race, Count Michaela."

The elevator closed and ascended.

"Count Michaela...I am the blood sucker?... Me?...No!...I am just a sucker!...Fifteen years I dreamed of you...What an idiot I was?...You are not getting away with this nonsense."

He looked for the staircase, took off, and ran up to the eighteenth floor. His training gave him great speed

98

and stamina. He arrived at the floor just as Lisa stepped out of the elevator.

"Lisa...Lisa..." said Michael.

"What?" said Lisa.

"You see this damn photo of yours?"

He was about to rip it up.

"Don't you dare rip it up? Don't you dare forget me!" Said Lisa

Michael stopped short of tearing the photo. He finally perceived the deep anguish he caused Lisa.

"What the hell am I doing? Everything is finished...I blew it. Pops. You. The Future....Maybe I am a bloodsucker?", said Michael.

He placed the photo in his shirt pocket over his heart.

"Even if you married me I would be taking you away from another man who loves you. Hurt someone else to save someone else, even to save Pops, which would go against everything he stood for.

Michael stood in silence realizing that Simon won. It was checkmate.

"What are you doing to me?" said Lisa. "You stir my emotions. Then you act like Sir Gallant. All noble and self-sacrificing...Did you think about me? I am not exactly a spring chicken. I waited all these years to have children with you, and now I maybe too old. So you don't tell me about self-sacrifice. And my mother passed on years ago...that's right she passed on... and never saw her daughter married with children because I waited for you. So please don't you dare tell me about your wants and needs...Go home, Michael. Go home. Good luck in your Race."

Lisa unlocked her apartment door and entered.

Michael remained standing, loathing himself.

For the first time in his life he accepted the reality he created and all the hurt he caused others.

He fixed his mind on the Race. It was the only thing he had left that could bring back his honor for his failed life.

"At least I'll give Pops something to be proud of", he said to himself. "...Come on, Michael. Let's run the Race."

He took off to the Triathlon.

Lisa was lying on her bed sobbing.

In three days Michael and Lisa would be separated forever.

# Chapter 19

The streets were packed with thousands of cheering spectators. Everyone's focus was on Michael and Danny. The racers straddled their bicycles as the support crews made their final inspections and recommendations.

Danny was seated in his specially made wheelchair fitted with three wheels, two in the back and one in the front. The design was modeled after a sports utility three-wheeler; it was slick, fast, light, and very maneuverable.

"I see Michael running towards us.", said Danny to Uncle Leo and the Old Timers.

Everyone was at their wits' end about Michael's whereabouts, especially Uncle Leo and Danny. They wanted to know if he succeeded or not with Lisa.

Michael didn't want to tell them what occurred. He was afraid that it would end the Race before it started.

"Well. How did it go?" said Uncle Leo.

"Made an inroad. We'll see...Lets' Race for Pops!" said Michael.

"Proud of you, boy." Said Uncle Leo. "Lets' do it."

With great pride Mom approached from the sidelines carrying a pouch. She slowly removed a folded banner and handed it to Michael. Surprised, Michael unfolded the banner; it was Pop's platoon colors embroidered with "82nd Airborne Captain Jake". Michael tied it to the pole at the back of Danny's wheelchair. It was flying high and proud.

Taken aback and moved, Uncle Leo, Sam, Mel, and Frank stood at attention and saluted. A moment later the crowd stood silent, saluted and broke into clapping, shouting, "For Capt. Jake".

Michael looked around at all the people cheering his father's name, overwhelmed by the gesture. As he turned he caught sight of his Public Shelter roomies, Bowery Bum Buddies, and the Subway Musicians friends he made over the years. Among them were Billy and Sid. He was their hero. To them Michael vindicated their lives of hellish suffering. He was one of them. He made it out of the dungeon and back to society. In a certain way they depended more on Michael than even Pops depended on him. At least Pops had a life. Most of these poor wretches were talented, intelligent, charming, and broken people that couldn't keep up with life's demands. They were Michael's most enthusiastic and heartfelt fans.

"Well, Pops. Win or lose, I am going to make your name known forever," Michael said to himself.

"Ladies and gentlemen", said the announcer. "Thank you for coming to the Triathlon and showing your support, care and cooperation. And we want to especially thank all of our amazing athletes competing today. At the sound of the gun the Race will begin. On your mark, get set. Go!"

The gun was fired.

The racers took off to the exuberance of the wild crowd.

"Pace yourself. You were up the whole night." Said Danny.

"I am", said Michael.

Pedaling hard but in good form, they approached the rough terrain of the race.

102

Overhead were flying the sportscasters' and police surveillance' choppers.

Michael began to slow down, his breathing became heavier and his concentration lessened. The lack of sleep began to affect him.

"Focus, Mikey. Focus," said Danny.

Michael tried but he was losing control over the bicycle.

The wristwatch alarm sounded off.

"Oh no", said Michael.

"What is that?" asked Danny.

The earth began shaking, darkness descended upon the terrain, and gusts of ferocious winds approached.

"What's happening?" said Danny.

Several racers fell to the side while others stopped in their tracks.

"Pull over," said Danny.

"Simon's legions are approaching. Take cover," announced the wristwatch.

"Racers. Everyone pull to the side. Major storm system is about to hit us. Pull to the side now," ordered the police surveillance pilots. Simon had manipulated the weather to isolate Michael and Danny.

Seeing a strange image in his side mirrors Michael briefly turned back to get a better look. It was the Demonic Shadows sent by Simon.

"Oh no. It's Simon's gang."

"Find a cave," commanded the wristwatch.

"Where?" said Michael.

Danny spotted one.

"To the right," said Danny.

"I see it," said Michael.

The Shadows were gaining on them. Michael gave full pedal and "blasted" towards the cave and entered.

"Preparing transport," announced the wristwatch.

Michael dismounted the bicycle.

The Transporting Tower of Light appeared.

"Twenty seconds to transport Michael Winston," announced the wristwatch.

"What about my brother?" said Michael.

"Fifteen seconds to transport Michael Winston."

Terrifying sounds were preceding the Demon Shadows.

"I am not leaving Danny behind."

The outlines of the Demon Shadows' streamed into the cave entrance.

Michael unstrapped Danny from the chair's seat belts.

"Eight...Seven..." announced the Wristwatch.

Swiftly removing him from the wheelchair, he unknowingly tore the computer voice linkup. Neither yet knew that Danny lost his means to communicate.

Michael carried Danny to the Tower of Light as the Demon Shadows entered the cave wielding swords.

As the Demon Shadows plunged their swords into Michael and Danny the Tower of Light transported them to Mr. Levy's conference room.

Mr. Levy and the Counsel were busy planning a counter strategy to outmaneuver Simon.

"Mr. Asher. Please take Danny," said Mr. Levy.

Mr. Asher lifted Danny, carried and placed him in a chair alongside the roundtable. His body was convulsing as it straighten out from all the years of paralysis.

"Why did you bring Danny? The transport only called your name," said Mr. Levy. "Do you know what you did?"

"I saved my brother," said Michael.

"I hope so."

"What is happening with Simon? He broke his word. Isn't this against all the rules of angels and celestial beings?" said Michael.

"I don't understand. In all the eons of history I have never seen Simon behave like this. There is a madness in him none of us can explain," said Mr. Levy. "We have less than minute to transport you to your father's location in the forbidden zone. That is where Simon is holding him. You have to make your father talk to you. Only he knows the reason for Simon's wrath."

"Fine. Lets do it," said Michael.

"I am going to," said Danny as he stood up from the chair. For the first time in his life Danny was on his own two feet. An emotional avalanche overcame his being, as well as it overcame Michael, he was seeing his little brother talk, walk, and speak up.

"Don't be surprised. There are no physical limits in the spiritual world. As for you accompanying Michae,l I am sorry," said Mr. Levy.

"Pardon me, sir," said Mr. Seth, one of the counsel consultants. "But it might be a good idea. Since both have the same parents, Simon's tracking system won't be able to register the difference, unless he's in close proximity. This will give Mr. Winston the diversion and time he needs to speak to his father."

"Fine," said Mr. Levy. "Gentlemen. Prepare transport. Michael. You and Danny are about to enter the Forbidden Zone. No celestial being can enter it. Your father is the only human to enter and survive. Since you and Danny are his children you possess the same makeup. Use your watch as a guide to find him. Good luck to both of you."

Michael and Danny stood side by side. The Tower of Light appeared and whisked them away to the Forbidden Zone.

# Chapter 20

Entering the Forbidden Zone, Michael and Danny were astonished by the vast emptiness and desert like wasteland conditions. It looked like an area devastated by hundreds of megaton atomic bombs. Its noises howled the haunting sounds and eerie music of doom, chase, and a perpetual manhunt, a place where the soul of man was forever on the run. A dimension of realized imagination where music took the place of mere sound and where the avant-garde and terror was the norm.

No celestial beings were allowed to enter since they possessed only pure thoughts. The Forbidden Zone would induce fear and unbridled thoughts resulting in self-destruction. Only a human being of an extraordinary caliber, with a balanced mixture of pure and impure forces, and experienced in free choice might have a chance to beat the odds.

"I know this place. I have seen this before." said Michael.

"It's like a scene from the Planet of the Apes," said Danny.

"Yeah. You're right. Is this what the world will look like when we really blow it up one day?" said Michael.

The wristwatch tracking system began functioning.

"That music is horrifying. It's like a composer is writing out the soundtrack in real time. Wow, a world where music accompanies reality. This is cool," said Danny.

"It's good to hear your voice again. Mom always imagined you had a beautiful voice. Maybe we can record your voice on my digital recorder," said Michael.

"Mom deserves to hear my voice," said Danny.

Michael nodded in agreement.

"She deserves a lot of good things," said Michael. "Ok...lets' go."

Running quickly along the tracking device's path, they managed the Forbidden Zone well. Approaching the area where Jake was held captive, the tracking system began beeping.

"Alert. Demon Shadows," said the wristwatch.

"Go ahead. I'll divert them," said Danny.

"Be careful. If they can take out Mr. Benjamin, they can take you out too," said Michael.

"Who?" said Danny.

"An angel," said Michael.

"Don't worry about me. Just go," replied Danny.

Danny headed to the "North", and Michael headed to a secluded half-tropical rainforest, half-desert area.

Running quickly, he saw a light in the distance outlining a silhouette of a man hanging from a tree.

Coming closer, he recognized the shape of the man. It was Pops hanging from a vine-like noose.

"Pops. Pops."

Michael tapped the watch, pressing all the buttons. A fiery beam shot out. Inadvertently he shot at the surrounding trees, setting them ablaze. He managed to aim the beam on the branch Pops was hanging on and cut it, causing Jake to fall.

Michael removed the noose.

"Pops are you ok? The fires are giving away our location. Can you walk?"

Jake nodded "yes".

They headed towards Danny's direction.

"Hey, you got a haircut, and your beard. You look good", said Pops.

The sounds of the Demon Shadows were closer.

"There is a cave over there," said Jake.

Entering the cave they waited until the Demon Shadows passed. It was the same cave that Michael and Danny ran to seek shelter from the storm. It was the cave's spiritual parallel.

"We're back," said Michael.

"Back where?" said Pops.

"Danny and I ran for cover..." said Michael.

"Simon is after Danny? That son of a...", said Pops.

"We were about a half an hour into the triathlon," said Michael.

"What?" said Pops.

"I have to do five things to get you out of the Pit; four of which are for myself, and one with Danny. Clean up. Harness my talents. Get a job. Find a wife. And do the Race with Danny," said Michael.

"You're kidding me," said Pops.

"That's why the haircut and shave. I began to shoot video blogs. I even got hired to shoot. And now we are running the Race." said Michael.

Pops was in disbelief. Michael was functioning like a normal man.

"You won't believe who I have to marry...Lisa Hoffman."

"Lisa?" said Pops.

"Hey Pops. You won't believe this. Look at your hands," said Michael.

Jake was rejuvenating. The cave possessed an age reversal force.

As the moments passed Jake was gradually

becoming younger, stronger, and healthier.

Pops wasn't as excited as Michael. He knew it wasn't permanent.

"Man. You are really getting younger," said Michael.

"Ok. Calm down. Lets focus for a moment. You have to marry Lisa?" said Pops.

"But that ain't happening. She's getting married in three days", said Michael. "I am not taking her from another man."

"You did the right thing," said Pops.

"That's why Mr. Levy sent us here to outmaneuver Simon. We need to know why Simon is so hell bent in destroying you. It has to do with War." Said Michael.

"The War? What does it have to do with the War? That's doesn't make sense. What about the million reasons?" said Pops.

"The million reasons. I am trying to do my best. You're blaming me too," said Michael.

"I am not blaming you...What about the war?" said Pops.

"Forget the War for a second. You see I am trying my best. Why did you bring up the million reasons?" said Michael.

"Forget about it. That's not the issue. Otherwise, why would Simon still be after me?" said Pops.

"Come on Pops. That is the issue," said Michael.

"Michael. Get a grip," said Pops.

"It has to do with day I saved Leo," said Pops.

"I saw the file," said Michael.

"Get rid of it and Simon will be off my back," said Pops.

"Simon got rid of the file," said Michael.

"And he still is after me?" said Pops.

"He said you had to do the Race?" said Pops.

109

"Yeah," said Michael.

"Son of a weasel. He is clever. He set you up. He used your free choice and concern for me against you. You need to get out of the race. If not, he'll do to you what he did to me," said Pops.

Michael was blaring with anger at Pops' insistence that he not race. He felt that Pops had no confidence in him.

"You're doing it again. I don't believe this." said Michael.

"What?" said Pops.

"I really don't believe this. It's Malibu all over again. You didn't encourage me then and you are not encouraging me now," said Michael.

"I don't believe it. Children. You're damned if you do. And you're damned if you don't," said Pops.

"Oh. Come on, Pops. Take some responsibility," said Michael.

"I am. Why do you think I am going to Pit?" said Pops.

"You just said because of the War," said Michael.

"That's part of it. The rest is because of you," said Pops.

Michael cringed to hear the truth from his father in such blunt terms and tone. It was the first time that Pops held nothing back.

"After you losing the film competition in Malibu...", said Pops.

"I should have won. Always pressure. What the hell was wrong with the committee? Why couldn't they wait another five minutes? Just another five minutes", said Michael. "Remember Pops? Everything looked so good. Hollywood was going to call. I was going to be the next

110

Orson Welles. John Houston...Yeah right. Why couldn't the committee wait five lousy minutes...I told you to drive faster. What was the big deal driving faster?"

"A little faster. You were a manic that day," said Pops.

"Stupid rules. Thank you, Mr. Winston," aid Michael, mimicking the committee members. "There is always next year Mr. Winston. Rules are rules, Mr. Winston. This is a competition, Mr. Winston."

"I told you not to wait until the last minute. Always the hare and never the turtle." Said Pops. "You thought you were Orson Welles. You had the whole semester."

"Well. I could have been Welles." Said Michael.

"That was always your problem. You could have been this. You could have been that." Said Pops.

Michael was fuming with rage.

"I see you want to hit me. Don't you?" said Pops.

Pops' body had reverted to his early thirties.

"Well, boy. I am young again. Come on, boy. Fight me man to man," said Pops.

"Don't do this Pops," said Michael.

"Or what? You can't kill me. I am dead already," said Pops.

"You are my Pops," said Michael.

"I give you permission. Come on. Lets' see what you are made of. At least you won't have any claims against me after I am gone," said Pops.

"Alright. Come on, War hero. Just remember I have lived on the streets for the last fifteen years. Don't expect a clean fight," said Michael.

"Well, boy. I fought against Nazis. Don't expect a fair fight either," said Pops. "You always wanted to know what kind of fighter I was in the War. Now you will see."

111

"Let's do it, Pops!" yelled Michael.

Michael charged Pops with all his force.

Grappling, punching, flipping and both using dirty tactics, father and son lashed out against each other with all their penned up frustration, anger, guilt, and love for each other. Pops was impressed with Michael's fighting abilities. But he was saddened too. He understood how much fighting Michael had done to survive on the streets. And Michael finally had the opportunity to see his father's great skills.

Both exhausted, Michael fell on Pops' neck and began to sob. He was fighting himself more than fighting Pops. And that is what Pops wanted him to realize. Michael saw himself clearly.

"Do you know how many years I lost? How many opportunities I missed? How many millions of things I could have done with my talents. I am a bum, Pops. A bum. I live in a cardboard box. A card box! I am a middle-aged man and I live in a box. No wife. No kids. No career. Why didn't you push me after Malibu?" said Michael.

"I didn't push you? After Malibu who carried the Bolex 16 mm camera when you tried to shoot another short? I pushed you but you didn't want to be pushed." said Pops.

Pops was beginning to age again but neither paid attention to it.

Michael thought about Pops' words.

"Fine, Pops. I admit it. I didn't want to be pushed", said Michael. "But what am I going to do now....I love Lisa so much. In three more days she will be someone else's."

"Listen to me", said Pops. "You are great man, with great talent. I believe in you. You make the Race. If Lisa is truly yours, the Heavenly Court will figure out a way so that nobody will get hurt."

"She is not going to marry me. I sucked out her soul", said Michael. "I caused her too much pain. I am a bum. I'm going to die a lonely old man...I wish I was dead."

Michael fell to the ground, placed his head on his knees, covered his head with his hands, and rocked back and forth. He was near having another nervous breakdown.

Pops was aging rapidly.

"Simon. Simon.", Pops yelled. "Leave my son alone. I will relinquish all my good deeds, all my heavenly merits I gained in war and life. Just leave my son alone. Stop tormenting him."

Danny had found and entered the cave.

"Pops," said Danny.

Pops was overwhelmed to see Danny standing and talking.

"All my life I dreamed to see..." He began sobbing.

They grabbed each other and hugged.

Pops guided Danny away from Michael, who was now talking to himself.

"Danny. You look and sound good. Listen to me. Don't let Michael fail. He needs you. Be his spirit."

"He needs me? Fifteen years? And he needs me," said Danny.

"Yes. Do it for me. I can take the Pit. But I can't take Michael in torment," said Pops.

The wristwatch alarm sounded off.

"Simon is in the vicinity. You must head to the Mountain", commanded the watch.

Simon's voice sounded in the winds.

"Jacob Winston. Jacob Winston. Prepare yourself," said Simon.

A long sinister and evil shadow shaped in the form of a hand slowly emerged into the cave. It leaned on Pops and began to rip him to pieces.

Danny tried to fight off Simon.

"Your father made his choice. It is done," said Simon.

"The dead have no choice. Only the living does. That's what Mr. Levy said", Michael said to himself. "The dead have no choice. Only the living....the dead have no choice. Only the living.", he repeatedly mumbled until it clicked inside. He had a way out, and sprang to his feet.

"Hear me, Simon. My father is dead. And the dead have no choice. My father agreed to nothing. Only the living can choose. And I choose to run the Race."

Simon instantly lost his grip, letting Pops fall to the ground. The excruciating pain had aged Michael terribly.

Michael ran over to Pops, placed his arms underneath, and lifted him gently off the ground.

"Come on Danny", commanded Michael.

They exited the cave and headed to the Mountain towards the horizon. Pops was now back to being a frail old man, thin and weak. His mind was lucid but his eyes looked puzzled. But he knew his beloved son, who he longed for years, was carrying and protecting him. He smiled as a tear rolled down his cheek.

Simon and the Shadows were chasing them, trying to prevent their ascent to the Mountain. But every time Michael would look to his father's eyes he only gained strength and determination. Michael had become a man. He had realized that his father was elderly and it was about time that he acted like the son he always should

114

have been.

At the top of the Mountain, Michael and Pops gazed into each other's eyes.

"Pops. I give my word as your son, you will not go down to the Pit."

Pops placed his frail hand on Michael's face, and gave him a slight caress and tap of confidence.

At that moment, a fortress rose from the ground, enveloping Pops, blocking Simon who was a moment away from grabbing him.

The Tower of Light appeared and whisked Michael and Danny back to the cave and back into real time.

"Danny. Come on," said Michael.

He turned and saw Danny on the ground, helpless, as his body and soul were reunited, returning him to his former physical state.

Michael ran over and turned Danny on his side. They stared into each other's eyes. Michael blinked. Danny returned a blink too. Michael nodded.

He understood Michael didn't succeed in finding out Simon's reason.

He lifted up Danny and carried him to the cave's entrance. They waited for the storm to subside.

Unexpectedly, an explosion of fierce lightning and thunder struck, increasing the downpour and sending Michael into a rage.

He stepped out of the cave, carrying Danny into the storm.

He tried to reach the bicycle as he slipped and fell several times. Wild, Michael began to lash out against the rain in a torrent of momentary madness.

"Bring rains and bring down hail for I have seen madness abound and drank from its burning well. A fool thou hast made me to lie in shame and unjustly blame

115

father, mother, and brother. But know now that in my heart no love that I love shall depart. Behold, for the Creator off Heaven and Earth knows of my worth. So come fate and meet your mate."

With conviction, energy, and power running through his veins he brought Danny to the wheelchair, set him in, and proceeded to attach the computer voice link, only to realize it was damaged. He faced Danny.

"Danny. The voice link tore. I'm going to adjust the bike mirror in your direction. We'll talk to each other like when were kids," said Michael.

They blinked to each other.

Michael adjusted the mirror, mounted the bike, and struggled to pedal through the mud. "Damn this," said Michael.

He dismounted, tried to pull the bike out of the mud but to no avail.

"Danny. It's too hard. We got to wait it out."

Danny blinked twice.

"What do you mean, no?"

Danny opened his eyes wide.

"What do you mean that's the point?"

Danny closed his eyes for a moment and opened them wide.

"It's a trick. You're right. That's what Simon wants."

Danny blinked once in agreement.

"No one is going to stop us. No one!"

He mustered his strength, pulled the bike out of the mud, mounted it again, and tried to pedal again and again.

A moment later the stormed stopped.

"You were right. It was a trick."

"Two days. Sixteen hours. And Twenty minutes", announced the wristwatch.

Slowly at first, and then in droves, the other Racers came out of hiding, passing Michael and Danny.

Michael and Danny gave each a blink and took off. They were back on track.

# Chapter 21

Lisa was watching the Race on her mobile phone during the taxi ride to the bridal store. She had to make some last minute changes to the dress. Of course she focused on Michael and Danny, but she felt numb, as if she was about to go under the knife.

Michael was pedaling heavily but with determination. The chain broke, snapping and cutting his leg. Bloody, he dismounted.

He quickly limped to the supply pouch attached to the wheelchair, removed the tools and scours for the chain. He made eye contact with Danny, drawing strength from his encouraging blinks.

Fixing the chain, he also felt the same numbness as Lisa.

Each entered into a trance. Both were transported into the other's mind and experiences. Lisa "saw" and felt Michael's last fifteen years. And Michael "saw" and felt Lisa's fifteen years. Lisa felt his love for her, his sense of abandonment, hardship, and fear of living on the streets. Michael felt her love for him, her sense of betrayal, sorrow, and hopelessness after she lost her mother. As the trance wore off both were ashamed of themselves for doubting, resenting, and not going the "extra mile" for the other.

The taxi arrived at the store. As she stepped out of the cab she received a text message, "I didn't know all the pain I caused you. From the bottom of my heart I apologize...Michael." She immediately replied, "I am sorry for not being there for you. You will always be my hero...Lisa."

She entered the shop and Michael continued the Race.

Night had arrived and the Racers were camped in a wooded area, which was illuminated by campfires lit by the Racers. Michael and Danny had their fire as well. Both were covered by blankets and very exhausted.

"Not a word. Not a word from Mr. Levy. Not even his assistants. We're on our own. Tomorrow morning they will bring the cable for the voice box," said Michael.

Within minutes both fell asleep.

The Race sirens woke up the Racers as the dawn broke. Quickly everyone got ready. Most of the Racers had taken off.

Danny was blinking a message.

"We can't wait for the cable. We are losing time."

"Ok", said Michael. "We will get the box at the next destination," said Michael.

Rapidly Michael packed up camp, put out the fire, mounted the bike, and took off.

Racing through the open highway, the view along the Hudson Valley was breathtaking. Michael and Danny were having a fabulous time. Each was proud of the other, especially Danny.

His resentment was subsiding. Finally he was getting back his older brother. Making great time and covering distance they arrived at Jones beach ready for the swimming event of the Race.

# Chapter 22

A half an hour had passed allowing all the Racers to setup. The beach was strewn with bikes and the waters packed with competitors. Danny was geared with a life jacket and secured in the raft. Uncle Leo had brought the computer cable. Danny's "voice" was back.

"Uncle Leo. We saw Pops. It's bad." Said Michael.

"When did you see him?" Said Uncle Leo.

"During the storm. The whole thing was a setup. Simon made the storm to divert us." Said Michael.

"And now you fellas are going into the water. If he has the keys to the weather he's going to drown you fellas," said Uncle Leo.

"We can't back out of the Race and we can't continue either," said Michael.

"Damn if you do and damn if you don't. Just like Pops always says," said Danny.

"The son of a lowlife outsmarted me...All these years I avoided marriage because I thought Simon would try to get my sons in retaliation for that day in '45. I was afraid to have children because of that....What a fool I was. Simon got two birds with one stone. Now I am an old man with no children, no descendants. And he still is going to get one of Jake's children. Boys. You can't do this. Let Pops be where he is. He wouldn't want you fellas to loose your lives for him." Said Uncle Leo. "I couldn't take to bury my nephews."

Michael and Danny looked at each other with great

concern and intent.

"And suppose we don't die then we gave up Pops. And your sacrifice not to have a family won't been in vain." Said Michael.

"No. Uncle Leo. We are going." said Danny.

"The death certificate hasn't been signed yet. We are Winston's," said Michael.

Uncle Leo conceded and wished them luck.

Michael secured the chain around his hips and onto the raft. Extending from the raft was a long pole with a mirror at the end. It enabled Michael to see Danny's eyes in case he couldn't hear his instructions.

"Ladies and Gentlemen. The second event is now about to begin. Contestants please take your places," said the announcer.

The gunshot was fired.

The Racers commenced swimming.

Swimming steadily and hauling Danny, Michael lifted his hand from time to time to inform Danny of his condition. One hand in the air meant he was doing fine. Both hands signaled he needed a break.

Unbeknownst to both of them the raft was losing air. Simon had outwitted them. He had sent one of his henchmen disguised as a raft inspector. While inspecting he punctured a small hole.

Across Michael's line of vision he saw a perplexing sight as if a Demon Shadow was dragging Pops along the water.

Pops was being dragged across an abandoned, lonely, dark, and evil terrain; he was being dragged into the Pit.

"Where are you taking me? We had a deal," said Jake.

In the far distance were the inferno flames, hellfire, and brimstone.

"Things change. From the jaws of defeat I snatch victory," proclaimed Simon.

Appearing on an air-like screen was the Battle Day in '45 file. Simon had it all the time.

"Remember this," said Simon.

The file commenced from the moment Jake jumped in the fire. Both Leo and Jake were screaming in agony. Simon appeared.

"Leo Winston. It's time," announced Simon.

For centuries Simon had taken human souls at their proper time. No one, since the beginning of time, ever was snatched from his jaws of death.

As Jake was watching his file, Michael and Danny appeared on a split screen. Both the day in '45 and the today's Race would be interlocked. At long last Simon would right the wrong done to him.

The raft became airless and began sinking. Danny was panicky. Bobbing up and down in the water Michael was trying to pull Danny from the raft.

"Let them live Simon," pleaded Pops.

"No. Jacob. Remember what you did to me?" said Simon. "Look."

Watching the day in '45, Jake saw Simon approach Leo. He was about to pull him into the fire when Jake jumped in front of Leo.

"Not my brother. Take me instead." yelled Jake.

Immediately the fire disappeared.

"What have you done?" cried Simon.

The file then ended.

"That day Leo belonged to me, Jacob. For nearly seventy years, I have lived with that defeat. Today my humiliation ends. Today you lose that merit. Today you lose both sons."

"Nooooo!" wailed Pops.

"Watch. Jacob," said Simon.

"Danny," yelled Michael.

Dragged down by the raft, Michael was drowning, too. Hastily, he released the chain and surfaced for air.

Simon appeared. "Too bad. Michael. But it is time to get back my honor," said Simon.

Simon submerged into the water and headed towards Danny.

"Not my little brother," shouted Michael.

Michael dived into the water and swam towards a nearly lifeless Danny. Simon turned the surrounding water into a water-like rope and placed it over Danny's neck. Slowly, he began to pull and strangle him.

Michael swam in front of Danny and placed his hand between the "rope" and Danny's neck.

"Take me instead," mouthed Michael.

"No!" screamed Simon.

Simon immediately disappeared, screaming and howling a maddening cry.

Michael grabbed Danny and pulled him to the surface.

Rescue guards were waiting to greet them.

Another raft was brought. Quickly Michael and Danny regrouped and continued the Race.

They finished the event. Michael had become like his father. He had gone through Fire and Water to save his brother. But there was still one more event, and Simon was not going to lose.

# Chapter 23

Night had come. The Racers were relaxing, sleeping or planning the next day's strategy. The final event would be a marathon. Michael and Danny were in their tent silent. Each one was attempting to understand the past two days. Danny had tasted the sweetness of movement and speech, and the terror of utter helplessness. Not until he experienced freedom did he realize his helplessness. But at the same time not until he obtained the ability to move did he understand how strong he was. He was amazed as to how he obtained such a spirit of competition to succeed, to move, to run even though he never ran until the day before. Though he knew he would never run again he was enthralled to know that he possessed an uniqueness, a passion that most able bodied individuals had no clue existed. And he was proud of Michael. He had an older brother that was now a hero.

Uncle Leo was at home with a photo of the woman he loved in one hand and a revolver in the other. Drunk, he was depressed to the depth of his soul. He now understood Simon's mark on his chest was a scare tactic, a terrorist threat, which prevented him from living life. He was saved that day in '45 only to lose the rest of his life. True had he died in the fires he would not have married and have a family but neither would have lived a tormented life of loneliness, worry, and lost love. He raised the revolver to his head and cocked the trigger.

"I should have died that day, Jake. And none of this would have been. All this suffering, for what?... All of this worrying, for what? Simon! Let go of my brother and nephews. Take my soul for them."

Simon appeared.

"Leo. Kill yourself if you want. I really don't care. You have been living on borrowed time since '45 anyhow. Your self sacrifice would be admirable but it won't change a thing."

"Why are you stopping me?" said Leo.

"I admire you Leo. You suffered so much for your family," said Simon. "If you sacrifice yourself now it would be pointless. There is no honor in pointless self-sacrifice."

Simon disappeared.

Leo was confused. He put down the gun. Gazing at the photo he fell asleep.

The woman in the photo was Margret Chauder. She was a widow and mother of three. Tonight she was assisting her niece, Lisa, helping her prepare for the wedding the following evening.

"He's quite the hero," said Aunt Margret. "Just like his uncle Leo."

"Wait a second. You knew his uncle," said Lisa. "How?"

"Your mother and I were nurses during the War. He was my patient. There were three of us taking care of the soldiers," said Margret. "Jes, your mother, and I. Jes married Jake. Of course your mother married your father. But for some strange reason Leo always put off marriage."

"Wow," said Lisa. "Winston's and Hoffman's knew each other."

How do you think you meet Michael all those years

ago?" said Margret. "Your mother and Jes thought you would be a good match."

"You're kidding me," said Lisa. "I always liked his parents. I never knew you knew his uncle."

"Yep. I am very impressed with Jes's boys. I find it amazing how tomorrow you're getting married and he will be finishing that race," said Margret.

"Yeah. It is a interesting coincidence." said Lisa. "Do you think Mom would have wanted me to marry Michael had he been ok?"

"You mean like the way he is now?" said Margret. "Maybe...yeah I am sure of it. But what was, was."

"You don't have to be so definite and say what was, was." said Lisa.

"You still have feelings for him?" asked Margret.

"Does it matter anymore?" said Lisa.

"Not really. Tomorrow night you will get married. And with the amount of girls sending their resumes to him he will get married too." said Margret.

"That's right. I will be married. And he will be married. And both of us will live happily ever after." said Lisa. Lisa was becoming upset.

"I need to take a break for ten minutes." she said.

She rose and went to her bedroom to lie down. Exhausted she fell asleep. Several moments passed.

"He is doing a good job. Isn't he?" said Lisa's Mom.

Mr. Levy helped Lisa's mom escape the World of Souls to speak with her.

"Mom is that you. Or am I dreaming?" said Lisa.

"It's me baby." said Mom.

"I missed you so much. It's been so many years." said Lisa.

"I know baby. From the time I got here your father has been my guardian angel so to speak. He misses you

126

too." said Mom.

Lisa began crying.

"We wanted to wish you a wonderful wedding and to tell you we will be there dancing with you." said Mom.

"Should I marry Bob?" asked Lisa.

"He is a wonderful man. But your soul belongs to Michael." said Mom.

"But I don't want to hurt him." said Lisa.

"He belongs to another soul." said Mom. "Talk to him. You'll see it's a girl named Alice. He knows her."

Lisa woke up. She was nervous, upset, and worried about her mental condition. She thought her mind was playing games on her.

"Michael. Why did you come back? You are driving me crazy."

She returned to the other room and continued preparing for the wedding.

Back at the tent Michael was contemplating the day. He felt different. He knew he had done something great. His mind was on Lisa. He took out his phone and texted her.

"I wish you only the best. Have a beautiful wedding and life. You deserve only happiness."

Lisa opened the text and began to cry. She felt that he didn't care for her enough; otherwise he would fight for her.

Mr. Levy could not tell Michael about Bob's true soul mate. Lisa had to be the one to approach Michael; otherwise if he approached her she would never erase the hurt he caused her from her soul.

# Chapter 24

Morning came with the wristwatch beeping, waking up Michael and Danny. Michael lifted the watch and saw the text.

"One more Race. See you there. Love, Simon."

Already Simon was playing mind games.

The morning siren sounded.

Within half an hour Michael, Danny, and the Racers were lined up at the starting line.

The wristwatch alarm sounded off, receiving a text.

"Michael. Too bad you can't carry the family weight. Love, Simon."

Michael pulled out the flag of the 82nd from the wheelchair, showed it to Danny, and tied it to the wheelchair's back pole.

"Simon. Today the Winston's' are sending you back to Hell!" said Michael.

"Damn right!" said Danny.

"Ladies and gentlemen. Today ends the Iron Man Triathlon. Racers take your positions," proclaimed the announcer.

The crowds were wild and none were more enthusiastic than Michael and Danny's fans. Mom, Uncle Leo, the Old Timers, the Shannon Pot Gang as well the homeless and handicapped kids were all there cheering them on.

"On your mark. Get set. Go!" declared the announcer.

The last shot of the Race was fired.

The Racers took off. Michael was pushing Danny with a steady pace.

"Be ready when I tell you to Thorpize it," said Danny. "We don't know when Simon will pull a fast one on us."

"Right," said Michael.

At the bridal shop, Lisa was adjusting her dress, assisting the wedding planner with seating arrangements, and still choosing the music list.

In came running Dina, Lisa's best friend.

"I don't believe this. Did you see the wedding invitations?" said Dina.

"What?" said Lisa.

"The wedding is scheduled for 11:30 this morning," said Dina.

"You're playing with me?" said Lisa.

Simon had manipulated the invitations and advanced the wedding by eight hours. He wanted to guarantee that just as the Race ended Lisa would be married off, insuring Michael's failure.

"This can't be," said Lisa.

"Well it is...The caterer just texted me. Several guests have arrived. Even Bob is there," said Dina.

"Fine. Fine. Lets get to the hall. We will finish the preparations in the car," said Lisa.

At the Race Michael was keeping his eyes focused on Danny. They were making good time until Michael's injury from the bicycle chain kicked in and started bleeding.

Michael tended to the wound and continued running. But the pain was too great.

"Thorpize now," commanded Danny.

Michael began to "Thorpize" the Race.

Simon won't take any changes. He was going to wreck havoc.

Lisa was now at the wedding hall.

Running past the kitchen she overheard the Race being televised on one of the employee's phone. The announcers were overwhelmed with Michael's courage and Danny's spirit. Lisa stopped and stood listening.

She took out her phone and texted Bob.

"Hi. Do you still have any feelings for Alice? Because I know she does for you."

Dina came looking for her.

"Come on. Get to the dressing room. I'll take care of the food or whatever you want," said Dina. "Just go. The guests are coming."

As she was being fitted in the dressing room Lisa was constantly looking at her phone waiting for Bob's reply.

Finally after a half an hour passed and receiving sixty texts from well-wishers, friends, and wedding personnel she received Bob's reply.

"How do you know?"

She quickly texted him back.

"I just know."

Bob replied, "Really."

"Really...Bobby...obviously you still have feelings for her...text her and find out...we should not do anything foolish..." she texted back.

After two minutes Bob replied.

"Lisa, you were right. She still does...I am very confused. I don't want to hurt you or her."

"Don't worry Bobby. I think she belongs to you. I am not hurt...I will tell the wedding planner that the wedding is canceled. Good luck in everything." Lisa texted.

"Dina! Dina!" said Lisa. Dina came running.

"Tell the wedding planner both Bobby and I canceled the wedding. I will talk to you later. I am going to get my bashert." said Lisa.

"What's bashert?" asked Dina.

"That's Kabbalah terminology for soul mate," said Lisa.

Lisa ran out of the hall, hailed a cab, and headed to the Race.

Almost three hours had passed and Michael and Danny were now a mile from the finish line.

"Seventy minutes remaining to the end of the thirty days," announced the wristwatch.

"Come on. Mikey. Push. Push. Thorpize it," said Danny.

Sweat was pouring down Michael's face and into his eyes. Wiping his face so hard with his sleeve he gashed his eyebrow. Blood was seeping down into his right eye disturbing his vision.

Nearly a half a mile from the finish line, a nearby Racer lost control and fell on Danny's wheelchair, severely damaging the right back wheel.

The wristwatch sounded off a received text.

Barely able to read it, Michael made out the text.

"Accidents do happen. Sorry. Simon."

"Bastard!" yelled Michael.

"Twenty-five minutes to the end of thirty days", announced the watch.

With only a quarter mile to go the back wheel fell off. Unable to push Danny, Michael swiftly unstrapped him, pulled him out, placed the voice box in Danny's pocket and began carrying him to the finish line.

Both brothers looked at each other's eyes with great intent.

"For Pops," said Michael.

131

"For Pops," said Danny.

Waiting at the finish line was Mom, Uncle Leo, the Old Timers, and the Michael and Danny's fans. Pandemonium filled the cheering crowd. The announcers were crazy with excitement.

Barely a thousand feet and in enormous pain Michael tripped and fell over a pebble on the pavement.

"Five minutes remaining. Four minutes and fifty-nine seconds remaining." announced the watch.

Lisa arrived at the Finish Line and pushed herself towards Jessica.

"You get up, Michael Winston. Get up." yelled Lisa. Mr. Levy made Michael hear her voice.

"Lisa. Lisa," he yelled.

Blood streaming down his face, he lifted up Danny and began limping towards the finish line.

"Three minutes and fifty nine seconds", announced the watch.

Michael was stumbling. Several times he fell but never letting go of Danny. Each time he got up and continued.

Michael looked at the watch and saw Pops being dragged to the Gates of the Pit.

"Pops."

"Two minutes and fifty nine seconds remaining."

At the finish line stood Mr. Levy, his Assistants, and Simon.

Falling thirty feet from the finish line Michael dragged Danny and himself towards the finish line.

"Michael! Michael!" chanted the crowd.

Both Mom and Lisa were crying.

"Come on, Michael," yelled Lisa.

Michael pulled himself and Danny across the finish line.

Lisa ran over to Michael.

"Yes Michael. I will marry you," said Lisa.

Michael looked at the watch. Pops was holding on to the gates, fighting to stay out.

"I need a ring. Someone give me a ring," shouted Michael. "Someone give me a ring."

The night before Uncle Leo was holding the ring he had bought Margret seventy years earlier. He had placed in his pocket while he was drunk. He remembered he had it and quickly removed it from his pocket.

"Sixty seconds to the end of the thirty days," announced the watch.

Michael tried to stand up but was too exhausted.

"Permission to help, Mr. Levy?" asked an angel.

"Permission granted." he replied.

The angel lifted Michael up and stood him upright.

Uncle Leo gave the ring to Michael. He could now barely see.

"Lisa."

She put her hand out, pointing her right index finger.

"With this ring I consecrate you as my wife in front of these witnesses. You belong to me and I belong to you," said Michael.

"PIT ABORTED! PIT ABORTED," announced the watch.

Michael turned around to see the face of the angel that helped him. It was Simon.

"Well Done. Mr. Winston. Well done, indeed," said Simon.

All the Angels were clapping.

While the crowd was cheering Michael, he and the Angels transported to the oval room he first met Simon.

Mr. Benjamin and Mr. Joseph were waiting for him.

"You're alive..." said Michael.

133

Pops stepped out of the shadow accompanied by Lisa's mother and father.

"You showed an extraordinary devotion to your father. Truly you have honored him," said Simon. "Have no fear about your father. His Heavenly place was assured long ago in that Great War and in the kind and good life he led. When the time arrived for him to take his place among the Greats he refused until you saved yourself. With the insistence of Lisa' parents, fine and upstanding people, themselves, we had to comply to their wishes that you and Lisa become the one soul you were originally created to be. We had no choice but to let you think your great father was going to the Pit. We hoped your incredible love for him would awaken the desire to save him in order to save you. Now you must return to Life."

"Take care of our daughter Michael." said Lisa's parents.

"I will."

Lisa's parents were then transported to their Heavenly place.

"Mikey. You did me proud. I always said you were a better man than me. And you proved it!" Said Pops.

Pops gave Michael a great hug.

"That should last you a lifetime." Said Pops.

"And make us some grandkids."

"Yes. Pops." said Michael.

"And give your Mom a kiss for me." Said Pops.

Mr. Benjamin, Mr. Joseph, and Mr. Levy then accompanied Pops to his abode.

Simon and Michael looked at each other with great respect and affection.

"Good luck. Or, as they say, Mazel Tov." Said Simon.

134

Immediately Michael was whisked back to the finish line encircled by the cheering crowd, chanting, "Good luck. Mr. and Mrs. Lisa and Michael Winston."

Michael and Lisa were whole again.

Made in the USA
Columbia, SC
22 January 2021

31406644R00076